SPEAK FOR ME

SPEAK FOR ME

K. R. Alexander

Scholastic Inc.

Copyright © 2022 by Alex R. Kahler writing as K. R. Alexander

All rights reserved. Published by Scholastic Inc., *Publishers since 1920*. SCHOLASTIC and associated logos are trademarks and/or registered trademarks of Scholastic Inc.

The publisher does not have any control over and does not assume any responsibility for author or third-party websites or their content.

This book is a work of fiction. Names, characters, places, and incidents are either the product of the author's imagination or are used fictitiously, and any resemblance to actual persons, living or dead, business establishments, events, or locales is entirely coincidental.

ISBN 978-1-338-80737-0

10 9 8 7 6 5 4 3 2 1   22 23 24 25 26

Printed in the U.S.A.   40
First edition, October 2022

Book design by Keirsten Geise

For those who struggle
to speak their mind.

6

Nomi Parker hated three things above all else: Spiders. Public speaking. And dolls.

Nothing scared her more than turning on the bathroom light in the middle of the night and finding a humongous hairy spider on the tile floor.

Nothing got her palms sweating like the idea of standing in front of her class to give a presentation—which made the fact that she wanted to be a theater star hard to imagine.

But neither of those compared to her fear of dolls.

When her friends had sleepovers, she made them put all their dolls in the closet. Or in another room.

Ideally she would have preferred to hide them all in another building. On the other side of town. Or on another continent.

When she went down the toy aisle, she had to look at the floor so she wouldn't catch sight of those beady doll eyes watching her lifelessly.

When a distant aunt had mistakenly bought her a doll for her eighth birthday, she'd hidden in her bedroom crying for the rest of the party. She hadn't come out until her dad had assured her the doll was gone. And never coming back.

She didn't know what was worse after that—having nearly been stuck with a doll or having all her friends laugh at her.

She didn't just hate dolls because they were creepy. Even though that was definitely part of it.

She hated them because whenever she looked at them, she started to wonder.

What would it be like to be stuck in a box like that?

What if every doll in the world could actually think, but they weren't able to talk and move on their own?

Sometimes she had nightmares about becoming a doll, unable to move or speak, unable to stop her owner when they decided to cut off her hair or put her in gross clothes or toss her to the family dog.

When she woke from those nightmares, her palms would sweat just like during a presentation, and her heart would race just as if she'd seen a hundred spiders in her bed.

The nightmares were bad. Really bad.

And they would soon become her reality.

1

"That honestly sounds like my worst nightmare," Nomi said, staring at Jenna in disbelief.

"Oh, come on," her best friend said. "You and me singing a duet? We'd be great."

"I don't know . . ." Nomi muttered.

Nomi looked from her friend to the poster taped to the school's wall. There were dozens of other posters papered all over the school, so everywhere she turned she was taunted with the same message:

JOIN THE TALENT SHOW
✶ ✶ ✶ BE A STAR ✶ ✶ ✶

And sure, that was her dream. Someday she wanted to star in the next *Hamilton*, to spend her nights under the lights of Broadway and her days exploring all the museums and cafés New York had to offer. She knew that meant practicing—and she did! She sang every night in front of her mirror and took voice lessons every weekend. She could play piano and recite scales by heart.

The trouble was, her stage fright meant that this was about as far as her training could go. Whenever she thought about auditioning for a play or taking part in a talent show, she started to hyperventilate. So far, the only people to see her perform had been her father, her voice coach, and her stuffed animals.

"You can pick the song!" Jenna urged. "And I'll choreograph a dance and—"

"Wait, we're going to *dance*, too?"

"Of course!" Jenna exclaimed. "Does Beyoncé just stand there? No. We gotta put on a show."

Nomi sighed. Mostly because she knew Jenna well—they'd been friends since they were both in diapers—and she knew Jenna would get her way.

Always. It was easier if Nomi just accepted it now. Putting up a fight never worked out in her favor.

"Okay," Nomi relented. "I'll do it."

The moment she said it, cold sweat broke out over her skin. Jenna didn't notice. She did a little cheer that made a few kids stop and stare at them, but she didn't mind. Unlike Nomi, she'd never had a problem being the center of attention.

And maybe that was why Nomi and Jenna had remained friends for so long—Jenna was always happy to take center stage, be it in a school play or in their small group of friends. Nomi was perfectly content to sink into the shadows, to take the bit part or listen while Jenna recounted their shared stories to the group. And if that meant Nomi didn't get the attention she secretly craved, well . . . there were worse things.

Like when Jenna got it into her head that they needed to do something ridiculously public together.

Like taking part in the talent show.

Jenna was Nomi's opposite in so many ways. Tall to Nomi's short, fair to Nomi's dark, loud to Nomi's quiet. Confident to Nomi's shy. Maybe that was also why Nomi was okay being in Jenna's shadow. She figured that someday, maybe, Jenna's confidence would wear off on her.

Usually Nomi would have tried to wriggle her way out of doing the talent show in a day or two, once Jenna had lost some of her enthusiasm. But it was their first year of middle school, and she secretly wanted to make a big impression on all her new classmates. She was a sixth grader now—surely she should be more confident and willing to put herself out there to follow her dreams. Besides, she knew if she waited, she would just chicken out for the next few years. And as for trying in high school? No way. She'd seen high school boys; no matter her age or year, she'd never be comfortable standing up in front of a crowd of them. Not unless she already had experience onstage.

Which meant it was now or never.

Jenna took Nomi by the arm and led her out of the school, already talking about the latest dance moves she'd seen online. Which felt a little silly to Nomi, since she still hadn't picked a song.

What am I even thinking? Nomi wondered. *Jenna will listen to whatever idea I have, tell me why it's probably not the best choice, pick another song, and try to make it sound like it was my idea in the first place. She's just letting me think I get to pick.*

Oddly, it didn't upset Nomi to think that. She was used to it.

And besides, Jenna knew what was best. She'd pick the right song. She always knew the right thing to do.

Always.

2

"I'm doing the talent show," Nomi muttered over dinner.

Her dad looked up at her, an eyebrow raised.

"The talent show, huh?" he asked. "I'm . . . well, that's great to hear, Nomi."

Nomi poked at her steak. Thursday nights were always steak night—her dad's specialty, and her favorite—but tonight she wasn't hungry at all. Not even for the mashed potatoes and gravy she'd helped make.

"Yeah," Nomi said. "Jenna said—"

"I should have known," he interrupted. "Of course it was Jenna's idea." He leaned forward and looked at her attentively. Nomi knew some dads never really paid attention to their daughters' friends, but her dad had been like this even before her parents had split and her mom had moved away. He'd always been the one to understand what her life was like. "Are you sure you want to do it? I mean, I know you're going to be a star someday! But I don't want you to feel rushed if being onstage makes you uncomfortable."

Nomi shook her head. "It's not like that," she said. Except it *was* like that. "We both want to do it. I've already picked a song, and she's going to choreograph a dance." She sighed and tapped her plate with her fork. "Even Mrs. Ulrich says I need to get over my stage fright soon."

Mrs. Ulrich was her voice coach. The kindly woman used to sing in the opera, so she knew what she was talking about.

"That's true," Nomi's dad said. "And I'm proud of you for facing your fears. But I also don't want you to let Jenna, well, you know."

"What?"

He sighed heavily. "Well, Jenna kind of walks all over you sometimes. I just want to make sure you're comfortable speaking up for yourself is all."

Nomi nodded, even though they both knew she wasn't

comfortable speaking up. Not at all. But that wasn't Jenna's fault. Nomi had always been shy.

"Anyway," her dad said, trying to change the subject, "I'm super excited to hear you sing. And you know we support you no matter what."

Nomi nodded. She knew what he meant: *If you want to back out, I'll support you, too.*

But she wasn't going to back out. Not this time. Not again.

That night, despite her previous convictions, all Nomi could think about was how she could get out of the talent show while saving face. When she was alone in her bed in the dark, it was easy for her to spiral, to worry about all the things that could go wrong. And quitting the show before she began seemed like the easiest way of avoiding all the horrible potential outcomes.

Maybe she could pretend to be sick a few days before? But then she'd feel bad for letting Jenna down, though—if she was being really honest—she knew Jenna would go onstage without her.

Or maybe she could say she had to go to a funeral and skip school?

Or maybe she could just skip school in general and move to a new town where she didn't know anybody. Maybe then she could find her voice.

Her mind raced, so she did what she always did when she couldn't sleep: She logged in to her social media.

The first thing she noticed was a new message, but she ignored it for a second to scroll.

She followed a bunch of celebrities and a few kids from school, a couple singers and actresses she admired. Photo after photo flashed by, images of famous people in famous places doing fabulous things, pictures of her friends and classmates somehow managing to be photogenic and fun no matter what, while she just felt frumpy.

It didn't make her tired, and it didn't make her feel better, but at least it kept her from spiraling in her own thoughts.

Then she scrolled past a sponsored post that nearly made her yelp.

It was an ad she'd seen in countless variations countless times for the past few weeks. An ad she had reported every single time as being "offensive" but that she still kept seeing—probably because the product was owned by the social media company.

They called her Emmy.

Emmy was a doll.

But not just any doll.

She was what they called a *smart doll*.

She could do anything a phone could do: play music, read out your texts and emails, make calls, take photos, browse the internet, and answer questions. All you had to do was link her to your phone, and she would become your best friend. The dolls all looked different: every ethnicity and body type, every gender, every age.

Every one was perfectly lifelike . . . and utterly terrifying.

Nomi immediately flagged the ad and refreshed her feed.

Even though Emmy vanished immediately, Nomi's palms were still sweating, and her pulse still raced.

After a few deep breaths, she decided she was done scrolling for the night. It was late, and she didn't think she could take any more mentions of dolls.

She checked her messages.

Jenna had sent a link.

The thumbnail showed . . . an Emmy doll.

But that wasn't the only thing that made Nomi's heart start racing again.

Jenna hadn't just sent a link to the doll, she'd sent a message.

They come out tomorrow! We HAVE to get some! They can be part of our act!

Nomi thought she was going to be sick.

Partly from the mention of the doll, but mostly because . . .

Well, mostly because she knew that Jenna always got her way.

3

The next day at lunch, all anyone could talk about at Nomi's table was Emmy.

"My dad promised he'd pick one up for me at lunch," Clarita said.

"My moms made sure mine was preordered and would be delivered before I got home," Jacqueline replied.

"What about you, Jenna?" Simone asked. "Are you getting one?"

Jenna blushed slightly, but she managed to hide it by laughing.

"Just one?" she joked. At least Nomi hoped she

was joking. "My parents said I'd have my pick over the weekend."

That, Nomi knew, was a lie. Money was tight at Jenna's house, and the Emmy doll cost hundreds of dollars. That didn't mean Nomi would put it past Jenna's parents to save up and get Jenna a couple dolls—they loved spoiling their daughter—but Nomi highly doubted it.

"I'd ask if you're getting one," Clarita said, looking at Nomi. "But I think we all know the answer."

Clarita had a huge doll collection. And that was why Nomi never stayed over at Clarita's house. Not anymore. Not after last time . . .

"What's that supposed to mean?" Jenna asked.

Clarita laughed cruelly. "*You* of all people know what I mean. Nomi's a scaredy-cat little crybaby. She wouldn't be caught dead with one of those dolls."

"Please," Jenna replied. "She's braver than you'll ever be. *We* are performing a duet for the talent show."

Jacqueline gasped, but Clarita just raised an eyebrow.

"Really? Both of you? You're not just going to have the doll sing in her place?"

Is that an option? Nomi thought hopefully.

Jenna roped an arm over Nomi's shoulders. Nomi

wasn't certain what she was more grateful for—the fact that Jenna had managed to change the subject from dolls, or the fact that she was sticking up for Nomi.

"Of course the both of us," Jenna replied. "We've already picked out the song and everything. What are *you* doing for the talent show, Clarita? Taking a selfie?"

"It would probably be more popular than whatever song you two screech out," Clarita retorted. And just to prove her point, she pulled out her phone, posed, and took a selfie.

Nomi had no doubt that it would have a few thousand likes before the school day was out. Clarita was beautiful, and her fashion was immaculate.

Jenna just laughed, and Jacqueline started talking about the show she was bingeing, and the whole talent show topic was behind them. Even though Clarita could be rude, she was still one of Jenna's best friends. Which Nomi supposed meant she was her friend, too.

Nomi didn't say anything while her friends talked. She just sat and listened and smiled and laughed at the right times. She ate her food. But although she was mostly paying attention, her thoughts kept drifting. Back to the talent show, back to her fear. And though it was chilly in the lunchroom, crisp and cool autumn air, she felt herself starting to sweat.

Now she *had* to go through with the talent show.

If she backed out now, they'd never let her live it down.

She glanced over at Jenna and wondered, briefly, if that's why her best friend had spoken up. Maybe it wasn't about standing up for Nomi—maybe it was all so Nomi would feel pressured to follow through.

But no. Jenna was her friend. She wouldn't do that.

Nomi was just letting her fear get the better of her.

Nomi and Jenna wandered down the street, surrounded by laughing classmates and music, everyone chatting about their weekend plans. Since next week was Halloween, most of those plans involved last-minute costume shopping, or a trip to the haunted house a few towns over. Nomi loved this time of year, partly because she liked all the decorations but mostly because she loved autumn—the bright red leaves, the excuse to finally wear sweaters again. Michigan autumns were the best. Plus, everyone here went all out for the holiday; the houses they passed were fully decorated with ghosts and ghouls, spiderwebs and grinning jack-o'-lanterns.

"Want to come over to my house to do homework?" Jenna asked. Jenna's backpack was loaded up with books, but Nomi wasn't bringing much home for the weekend. She'd already done most of the week's homework.

"Sure," Nomi said. She knew it was code for *help Jenna do her homework*, but she didn't mind. She liked helping. And being around Jenna.

"Great!" Jenna replied. "We can work on our routine, too. I'm so excited. We're totally going to make Clarita eat her words."

Nomi felt herself blush—maybe because of Jenna's confidence, maybe because any mention of the talent show made her panic.

"Have you picked out the song?" Jenna asked.

Nomi nodded and told her which one. It was a pop song she knew Jenna would like, and Jenna's eyes lit up when Nomi said it.

"That's going to be *amazing*," Jenna said. "I can already picture the dance routine."

She started dancing around as they walked, making Nomi giggle. Then Jenna stopped and very nonchalantly said, "Hey, mind if we run by the store quick?"

"No problem." Nomi figured Jenna needed to pick up groceries for dinner, or snacks for after if they were going to do an impromptu movie night.

But Jenna didn't lead her to the corner store they normally went to. She walked a few blocks in the other direction, toward one of the larger department stores.

"What do you need to get?" Nomi asked as they walked through the glass doors.

Jenna winked at her. "You'll see."

Nomi didn't like that look. That look always got her in trouble.

Her fears didn't ease as Jenna expertly wound her way down the aisles.

Toward the back of the store.

Toward the toy aisle.

Nomi heard them before she saw them:

the perfect voices,

the singsong phrases.

Then she and Jenna rounded the corner, and Nomi came face-to-face with a display of a hundred Emmy dolls.

Nomi stopped dead in her tracks.

Staring.

They were all staring.

Trapped inside their boxes and
    S
       T
          A
            R
              I
                N
                  G.

"What are we doing here?" Nomi whispered.

"You're getting us Emmy dolls," Jenna replied.

"But . . . what? I can't afford them."

And I don't want one!

Nomi made the mistake of focusing on one of the dolls. It was looking back at her, as if listening in.

Nomi shuddered and looked away.

That glint came back to Jenna's eye.

"I know," Jenna said. "Neither can I. But you're going to help me steal them."

4

Jenna had a plan.

Of course she had a plan.

And the plan involved her being the center of attention.

Nomi's best friend *needed* to be in the spotlight as much as she needed to breathe.

And as they made their way toward the dolls, that fact became clearer than ever.

"Oh, *wow*!" Jenna exclaimed loudly. She set down her backpack and headed to a table where two sample dolls were standing out of their boxes, on display. Like something out of a TV commercial, she picked up one of the dolls, looking it over and exclaiming, "They're so *lifelike*!"

On cue, one of the sales associates walked over with a big smile plastered on their face.

"Would you like to learn more about Emmy?" the associate asked.

Jenna nodded, and the associate proceeded to tell them everything they already knew about the doll: It could act as your personal assistant and best friend, could tell you about the weather and help decide if your outfit worked.

"In other words," the associate concluded, "it can do *everything*."

At least it can't walk, Nomi thought. She stayed a few steps away, watching it all with a sick feeling in her chest.

Then Jenna waved her over.

"Check this out," Jenna said.

She picked up another doll and handed it to Nomi. Nomi almost dropped it, but she held on. She also made sure to hold the doll facing *away* from her.

The back of its head wasn't so scary.

The back of its head wouldn't stare.

But why did Nomi feel it might turn its head at any moment?

Jenna continued to fawn over the doll she was holding, talking loudly about how excited she was for her parents to pick one up, musing about which one she wanted. She even tried to rope Nomi into the monologue, saying she couldn't wait for them both to have Emmy dolls so they could play together.

It was a loud enough display that everyone in the toy department was paying attention to her.

And when Jenna stepped backward into a large pyramid of Emmy boxes, *everyone* paid attention.

Jenna yelled out theatrically as she tipped over.

The boxes exploded around her, falling all over the floor and obscuring Jenna momentarily. The associates all rushed over, and Nomi dropped the doll she'd been holding to help rustle through the boxes, trying to find Jenna.

Jenna moaned and yelled out, and for a brief moment, Nomi worried her friend was truly hurt. Boxes flew as associates tossed them aside to find her, and all the while Jenna called out about wanting her parents and how much it hurt. The associates, clearly fearing lawsuits, quickly scrabbled to get her.

Finally they cleared away the boxes and helped Jenna to stand. She hunched over, wincing dramatically.

"My ankle," she whined. "I think I sprained my ankle!"

"Do you need to sit down?" asked the associate. "Do you want me to call someone?"

Jenna shook her head and started to breathe rapidly. It sounded like she was hyperventilating.

"No," she said. "I need to get out of here. I need fresh air."

"Okay, let's get you outside."

The associate looped Jenna's arm around their neck. Jenna grabbed a backpack from the ground, and Nomi—still in a daze, still wondering what had just happened—grabbed the other backpack and followed the associate and Jenna toward the front door.

When they reached the doors and walked past the sensors, the alarm went off.

Nomi froze in her tracks.

Jenna moaned in pain and breathed faster.

"Don't worry about it," said the associate. "Probably just my key card."

They walked through, and the alarms went silent, and then the associate was setting Jenna down on a bench and asking if she was *sure* she didn't need a family member called. Jenna assured them that it was fine, she just needed some fresh air and then she'd be okay. Her ankle was feeling better already.

The associate looked at Nomi, confusion clear on their face. Nomi just shrugged.

"I'll take care of her," Nomi said.

The associate went back inside.

The two of them sat there for a while. A few customers walked in and out, and some leaving looked at her with concern—they'd clearly seen what had happened in the toy aisle. But no one stopped to check.

"Are you okay?" Nomi asked.

"Totally," Jenna said. She flashed her a winning smile. "Pretty good acting, right?" She immediately twisted her face back into an expression of pain. "I think they bought it."

"I don't . . . what happened?"

"We did it," Jenna said.

"I didn't do anything," Nomi replied.

Jenna just laughed and nudged the book bag at her feet.

That's when Nomi realized that it was *her* bag. Jenna had picked it up rather than her own.

And even though Nomi's bag had been empty when she'd left school, it was now bulging. And Nomi knew it wasn't from books.

Jenna had used her bag to steal the Emmy dolls.

5

Nomi didn't say anything as they made their way back to Jenna's house. Not that that was particularly unusual, but this felt different. The silence was intentional. Her own form of screaming at the top of her lungs.

She felt betrayed.

Nomi hadn't stolen anything in her life. And she supposed, in a way, she hadn't *really* stolen the dolls. But she was an accessory to the crime. She was still guilty. And every step they took away from the store (Jenna, pretending to limp until they were a block away and out of sight), Nomi felt a little guiltier for not turning around and telling someone.

But what could she do? If she told on Jenna, Jenna would never forgive her or talk to her again, and all of their mutual friends would take Jenna's side, and Nomi would be alone. The whole situation made her clench her fists and grit her teeth. But if Jenna noticed that Nomi was upset, she didn't acknowledge it.

All she did was talk about how excited she was to have an Emmy doll.

"And don't worry," Jenna said at one point, "I made sure to get you one, too."

That comment made the anger in Nomi's blood freeze. At least for a moment. Because Jenna *knew* that Nomi hated dolls. Just as Jenna knew that Nomi never stole or lied or did anything bad.

Just as Jenna knew that Nomi would never speak up for herself.

Nomi remembered what her dad had said at dinner, and she wondered if Jenna was actually her friend, or if Jenna just considered her a fan. Part of her entourage.

Nomi felt her anger grow, but she didn't risk saying anything.

She was just being too sensitive.

They reached Jenna's house and went up to her

room. Jenna tossed Nomi's bag onto the bed and flopped down, kicking off her shoes before digging in. Nomi stood awkwardly in the doorway, watching Jenna warily. Even though she'd been in Jenna's room hundreds of times, she felt like she was entering unknown territory.

She didn't want to be here. Not with the bulging bag containing the Emmy dolls taking up the place on Jenna's bed where she'd normally sit. Not when she knew what was about to happen.

Jenna didn't seem to notice, though. She pulled out a box and tossed it over to Nomi. Nomi caught it out of habit, but she wanted to toss it right back.

The doll looking through its plastic screen was straight out of one of her nightmares.

The doll looked angelic, with big eyes and a sweet smile and curly brown hair. She wore a pale blue baby-doll dress and had shiny black shoes. It made her skin crawl. And it was hers.

"You know," Nomi said. She held the box away from her, like the doll inside was diseased. Or on fire. Or about to attack. "I don't need one. You can have her if you want."

"Don't be stupid," Jenna replied. She already had her Emmy out and was figuring out how to turn it on. "I don't need two of them. Besides, if we sync them, they can communicate with each other no matter where we are, so we can play even when you're home."

And oddly, that was enough—that one throwaway statement—to make Nomi's anger fade.

Jenna got the dolls not because she was selfish, but because she wanted to play with Nomi. Even when Nomi wasn't around. She hadn't gotten a doll for Clarita or Jacqueline. Jenna got the doll for *her*. Nomi *was* just being sensitive. Maybe it wouldn't be so bad after all.

It was just a doll.

If she could get over her fear of the stage, she could easily get over her fear of a doll. And who knew? Maybe it would work the other way around—if she got comfortable having a doll in the house, maybe she'd grow brave enough to do the talent show.

She sighed, set down her bag and took off her shoes, and joined Jenna on the bed. She pulled out her Emmy and turned it on. When it booted up, the strangest thing happened:

The doll's head spun
  all
    the
      way
  around.

A light flickered behind her eyes so quickly Nomi almost wondered if she had actually seen it.

"Creepy!" Jenna said, watching as Nomi's doll shuddered and began speaking gibberish.

Nomi had the urge to throw her doll out the window. She set it on the bed instead.

"Maybe yours is defective?" Jenna suggested. Because Jenna's doll had booted up without any strange movements or noises.

Nomi stared at the doll with dread growing in her stomach, but in seconds the doll's little plastic lips curved into a smile, and her creepy voice rang through the room.

"Hello! I'm Emmy! Let's be friends. What's your name?"

"N-Nomi," Nomi said.

"Hi, Nanomi," her doll parroted. "That's a pretty name."

Jenna howled with laughter.

"No," Nomi said, embarrassed. "It's not *Nanomi*. It's just Nomi."

"Okay, Nanomi. Great!" her doll replied. "Would you like to change my name, too?"

Nomi considered.

"Alice," she finally said. Alice wasn't a scary name. She couldn't be freaked out by a doll named Alice. Right?

"Great! I love that name, Nanomi. From now on, you can call me Alice."

Jenna chuckled, but she didn't say anything else about the mix-up over Nomi's name. She was too busy syncing her doll to her phone.

Nomi sighed and did the same.

In no time at all, they had the dolls turned on and synced to their phones. They downloaded Emmy's app and started playing around with all the cool and unique things the dolls could do.

"Check this out," Jenna said with a giggle.

She typed something into her phone. A moment later, Jenna's doll spoke in a childish, slightly robotic voice.

"Hey, Nomi, you smell like monkey farts."

Jenna laughed out loud, but Nomi groaned.

"At least *yours* got my name right," Nomi replied. She looked at her own doll, which was sitting beside Jenna's.

Alice was looking straight at Nomi. Those eyes . . .

Alice was *definitely* going to have to stay in another room tonight.

"Don't worry, Nanomi," Alice said. "You don't have to be scared of me. I'm your best friend." Her head rotated to look at Jenna, who wasn't paying attention, and then looked back to Nomi. "And soon," the doll whispered, "I'll be your *only* friend."

The doll hadn't said that.

There was no way the doll had said that.

Nomi told herself she'd misheard it. Because there was no way the doll could be threatening—that was part of its programming. To be a friend. A good friend: kind, pleasant, sweet. And threatening Jenna definitely wasn't sweet.

But Jenna clearly hadn't heard anything, which just made Nomi think that she'd made it up, that it had just been her own fear growing too loud in her skull.

Jenna thought the dolls were amazing. Not only could they play any song Jenna requested, but they could also project music videos from their eyes. Jenna spent a good twenty minutes dancing in the projection on her wall while Nomi laughed and eventually forgot all about the strange thing she wasn't so sure she'd heard.

Jenna even tested her Emmy on some of her homework, and the Emmy gave her all the right answers.

"How perfect is this?" Jenna asked.

Alice and Jenna's Emmy smiled.

Nomi felt herself smile, too. But when it was time to go, fear lodged back in Nomi's throat. The moment she left here, she'd be bringing the doll back to her house. To her room.

The doll was okay with Jenna and her doll around, but when it was just Nomi . . . No thanks.

"Why don't you keep mine here?" Nomi suggested, trying to keep her voice light.

"No way," Jenna replied. "We have to see how they work when they're apart. It'll be cool, I promise."

Nomi tried to hide Alice from her dad when she got home.

She had just as much luck hiding the doll as she did forcing Jenna to keep it.

Nomi *would* have been successful at keeping the doll hidden if Jenna hadn't taken the exact moment

Nomi walked in the door to make Alice call out, "Ring, ring! Jenna says she misses you!"

"What in the world was that?" Nomi's dad asked, coming into the hallway.

Before Nomi could think of a good lie, Alice followed up with, "Would you like me to reply to Jenna?"

"Your backpack's become very talkative," Nomi's dad observed.

"It's just something Jenna got for me," Nomi mumbled.

"Can I see?"

Nomi didn't see that she had any choice. Especially when Alice started saying, "Let me out!"

Had Jenna told her to do that?

Or was she doing that on her own?

Nomi shivered as she opened the bag and held it out to her father.

He peered in. "I thought you hated dolls," he said. Then, to her horror, he took Alice out of the bag and turned her around in his hands.

"Who are you?" Alice asked.

Nomi's dad chuckled. "I'm Nomi's father."

"Hello, Nanomi's father." Alice's head turned back and forth. "You have a lovely home."

Nomi wondered if the dolls had GPS that allowed Jenna to track her, or if there was a way Jenna's Emmy could show her what was going on. Jenna was probably cackling with laughter right now.

"I . . . I'm facing my fears," Nomi said. Which pretty much meant there was no way she could ask her dad to hide the doll in his room tonight.

Her dad looked at her and raised a quizzical eyebrow.

"Jenna got one for herself, too?" he asked. "These aren't cheap, and I don't imagine her allowance is much more than yours."

Nomi had been thinking up a cover story the entire walk home. It was flimsy, but she hoped it would work. "She had some extra money from her birthday and said this was my early present."

Jenna's birthday was last week—her parents had gotten her a new phone—and Nomi's was just before Thanksgiving.

"How . . . thoughtful?" her dad said. He held Alice out to her. Nomi had to force herself to take the doll back. "Are you sure this is the gift you want?"

"What do you mean?"

"I mean . . . well, you know."

Nomi *did* know. Of course she knew—Jenna was great at getting what she wanted and making it sound like it was your idea. But Jenna hadn't done that this time. She'd gotten the dolls so they could play together. It was a sign of friendship. Simple as that.

"I'm facing my fears," Nomi repeated. "Besides, she's not just like any doll. She's a *smart* doll. She's synced to my phone and can—"

"Oh, I know, I know," her dad said, waving her spiel aside. "I've heard the ads a million times. All my socials are covered with promo for it. It's clear they know I have a daughter."

He stuck out his tongue at Nomi, indicating what he thought about getting ads for dolls rather than something he'd be interested in. Like video games. Or the newest electric car.

"Hey, monkey butt," Alice said suddenly. Nomi nearly jumped out of her skin. "Jenna wants to play."

"That's going to get real old," Nomi's dad said with a sigh. "Tell it to watch its language."

Nomi just sighed dramatically in agreement and carried Alice upstairs.

7

If Nomi was able to set aside the fact that Alice was a doll—and a very creepy, realistic one at that—she could almost sort of see the appeal. She'd pretty much pushed aside what Alice had whispered to her earlier, telling herself that it was either a glitch, or Alice hadn't actually threatened to be her only friend. Which meant she was able to spend the rest of the night playing with the doll and, by proxy, playing with Jenna.

Alice could only move her head and arms and wiggle her feet, for which Nomi was grateful. The thought that Alice might run around on her own free will scared the daylights out of her. She had the doll propped up on her pillows, chatting with Jenna while reading through magazines, when Jenna's voice called out, "Oh! Look at this!"

A second later, Alice's eyes flickered like they had when Nomi had first turned the doll on, and the doll moved her head to the side. Nomi startled, edging back away from the seemingly possessed doll, when a beam of light shot from Alice's eyes and illuminated the wall.

She was acting as a projector.

On the wall, overlaid on top of Nomi's posters and paintings, she saw Jenna's face.

"This is so cool!" the doll said in Jenna's voice. "Now we never have to be apart!"

Nomi giggled and inched closer. Her heart swelled at Jenna's excitement. Once more, she thought to herself that the doll hadn't been a selfish move on Jenna's part—she wanted to use it to be closer to Nomi. Her dad was wrong about Jenna. Jenna was actually very considerate.

"Can you see me?" Nomi asked. "How do I do it?"

"You have to press her left hand three times. I finally read the instruction manual. Did you know she can also *control* any smart appliances you have in the house? I already have her set to turn on the lights and TV when I walk in the room. It's so cool."

Nomi grinned. She leaned over and reached out, took Alice's hand in her own.

She pressed Alice's palm.

Once.

Twice.

On the third time, Alice's fingers curled around Nomi's thumb.

Nomi yelped and lurched backward, making Alice topple to the side.

Jenna's projection flickered out.

"Nomi?" Alice asked in Jenna's voice. "Nomi, what happened?"

"I-I just . . ."

She stared at Alice in horror.

As the doll's head rotated

    around

        to

          stare

       at

     Nomi.

"Don't be scared of me," the doll said, this time in its own childish, robotic voice.

Nomi couldn't speak.

"Nomi?" Jenna's voice came out.

"I'm okay," Nomi managed. "But my dad wants me to go to bed, so I'll talk to you tomorrow."

"Okay . . ." Jenna said.

Nomi didn't want to touch the doll again, but she reached over and hit the off button on the back of its neck.

Then she scurried backward until she was pressed against the wall. She stared at her doll.

"Did you . . . did you just talk?" Nomi asked.

The doll didn't respond. It just stared at her with those glossy black eyes. Light flickered behind them.

The silence was almost worse.

Nomi was one hundred percent positive that she'd hidden Alice in her closet.

Under a pile of clothes.

Which were under a pile of stuffed animals.

Which were under a thick blanket.

Which was weighted down by her shoes.

She would have locked the closet door if it had a lock.

She. Was. Positive that the doll was safely hidden away.

Out of sight, out of mind.

Well, as out of mind as it could be when every time she closed her eyes, she saw its creepy smile staring back.

Did it really say those things to me? she wondered as she clutched the covers over her head.

Maybe it was Jenna playing tricks? That had to be it. The dolls were synced—Jenna could make Alice talk, just like Nomi could make Jenna's doll talk if she wanted. Not that she wanted to. She wasn't that type of friend. It was all a joke. All a perfectly logical part of the doll's design.

She didn't have anything to be afraid of.

Nomi told herself this repeatedly as she somehow managed to fall asleep. Even then, she didn't fully believe it.

She was positive she'd hidden the doll away.

Which was why, when she woke up Saturday morning to find Alice sitting on her bedside table, she nearly screamed.

Nomi slapped her hand to her mouth to keep the bone-rattling yell from ripping out. She stared at Alice in horror, and Alice smiled back at her.

The doll didn't move. The doll didn't blink. The doll was still supposedly off.

But Nomi knew that the doll was watching her.

Her phone buzzed, and this time Nomi *did* scream. Well, yelped. Just a little.

It was Jenna, texting to see if Nomi wanted to hang out. And also:

TURN ON YOUR DOLL!

It was the last thing Nomi wanted to do, but she knew that if she resisted, Jenna wouldn't stop pestering her.

And what was Nomi going to say?

That she was scared?

That the doll was possessed?

Jenna would just make fun of her and *make* her keep the doll on.

Nomi sighed, steeled herself, and reached over to pick up the doll.

Alice seemed to smile wider when Nomi held her. Alice seemed to be *warm*. But maybe it was just Nomi's imagination. Maybe the battery was overheating somehow.

Maybe the doll really was just defective.

She pressed the button on the back of Alice's neck, and the doll immediately blinked and squirmed, as if waking up from a long nap.

"Good morning, Nanomi," Alice said in her usual voice. "Did you sleep well? I sure did."

"Yeah," Nomi muttered. "Until you somehow snuck up to spy on me."

"I missed you, Nanomi," Alice replied. She reached up a hand. "I want us to be friends."

"Yeah, right," Nomi said. "And my name is *Nomi*. Got it?"

Alice nodded. Nomi doubted that the doll meant it.

And sure, it was just a toy, but she felt . . . better? Hearing that the doll wanted to be her friend, that she had missed Nomi. When was the last time Jenna had said something like that? When was the last time Nomi had felt appreciated by a friend?

Or heard?

Maybe Alice wasn't scary and evil like she'd first thought. Maybe Alice really did just want to be her friend.

The doll wiggled again, and a musical note chimed in the air.

"Nanomi, you have thirty new messages from Jenna. Would you like to hear them?"

Nomi groaned and flopped back on her bed. She kept Alice at arm's length.

"Fiiine," Nomi relented.

Alice began.

9

"I'm going to be brutally honest," Jenna said. "I really thought you would have thrown her out by now."

They were over at Jenna's house again, the dolls sitting on the bed between them. Nomi had just finished her voice lesson and was feeling pretty good—she'd nailed all the notes, and her teacher had said she was really improving.

At least, she'd felt good until Jenna brought up the dolls.

"Why would you think that?" Nomi asked.

"Well, I know you hate dolls," Jenna said. "But I'm impressed. You got over your stupid fear!"

It isn't stupid, Nomi thought, glancing at Alice. She still hadn't told Jenna that she'd found Alice on her table this morning. That she thought Alice had a mind of her own—and two legs that worked.

She'd never hear the end of it.

"Well," Nomi said instead, "I was thinking about what you said about fear, and I wanted to face mine, and—"

"Oh!" Jenna interrupted. "I almost forgot."

She pulled out her phone and typed something in, completely ignoring Nomi's hurt expression.

A moment later, Jenna's doll (still named Emmy) turned, and a projection lit up the wall.

"I was thinking we could do this routine," Jenna said.

Emmy started projecting a music video. It was a pop song that had been playing everywhere lately. Nomi had liked it at first, but she'd heard it so many times that she'd started to hate it.

It was also entirely different from the song she had picked out. Different melody, different tempo, different style.

Her heart sank as Jenna got up and started

mimicking the dance. She knew in that moment that they would be doing this song, even though it was out of her vocal range. And comfort zone.

Jenna seemed to notice Nomi's sullen look.

"Don't worry," Jenna said. "The moves aren't that hard. Here, come try. Emmy! Replay that song."

She dragged Nomi to standing and started coaching her through the moves.

Nomi wasn't able to keep up, and after half an hour of fumbling through practice, she was nearly in tears.

"Maybe we should try a slower song," Nomi suggested. *Like the one I picked out a few days ago!*

"No, don't be stupid. You'll get it. And if you don't, we can always, like, find some easier moves for you. You can be like the backup dancer or something. Hmmm, actually. Emmy, call Clarita!"

Nomi's chest constricted while the doll emitted a musical ringtone, and then Clarita picked up.

"Hey, Jenna," Clarita said through the doll. "What's up?"

"Come over," Jenna said. "We're rehearsing, and I think we need to make this a trio."

"Okay," Clarita replied, and hung up.

Nomi didn't know what hurt worse—learning that this performance was no longer going to be a duet with her best friend, or learning that her best friend had already connected to someone else's doll. After all, you could only make calls between two synced dolls, not to a regular phone.

"Sweet," Jenna said. "See? Now you don't have to stress out so much. If you can't do it, Clarita can cover for you."

Jenna smiled widely and started going through the routine again, this time not even bothering to try to teach it to Nomi, who just sat on the bed beside the dolls and watched.

She was sure that her Alice doll was watching Jenna, too.

And just like Nomi, the doll was frowning.

10

Nomi felt horrible for the rest of day and into the night.

Clarita had come over and bossed her around, and by the time they had finished rehearsing, Nomi was practically in tears. Clarita had taken her spot, dancing next to Jenna so Nomi had to be in the back.

And, worse, when Clarita had sung out a few lines, Jenna had exclaimed that her voice was perfect.

Clarita had taken Nomi's part.

Even though Nomi was *definitely* a better singer. She'd practiced harder. She wanted it more.

But when Jenna had asked Nomi if she was okay

with Clarita taking the part, Nomi had just nodded along without putting up a fight.

She also hadn't put up a fight when Clarita had synced up her Emmy to Alice. Not that it mattered— Clarita had Nomi's phone number and was on all her socials, but Clarita never talked to her. She probably wouldn't have done it if Jenna hadn't insisted, saying that this way they could *all be on the same page*.

"You're a loser," Nomi muttered to herself. She sat on her bed in the dark. It was late, and her dad was asleep, but she couldn't get her mind to quiet down enough to pass out. She just kept tossing and turning, thinking about how she should have stood up for herself. Thinking about how she wasn't facing her fears at all.

"You're not a loser," came Alice's electronic voice.

Nomi jolted and looked over. Alice was lying against the wall where Nomi had tossed her earlier. She didn't want anything to do with something Jenna had gotten her.

Especially something Jenna had coerced her into stealing.

She was also pretty sure she'd turned off the doll when she left Jenna's. She didn't want Jenna to be able to reach out to her. Not right then. Not when she was so upset.

"Thanks," Nomi said now. "But you're the only one who thinks that."

"That's not true," Alice replied. "You're talented and have a great voice. I love your voice, Nanomi. More people should hear it."

Nomi knew the doll was just a hunk of plastic and electronics. It probably had some sort of therapy function, to make kids feel better about themselves. But even though it was just a toy, Nomi had to admit that it was making her feel better. Even if it couldn't get her name right.

She slipped out of bed and walked over, picking up the doll and examining it in the dim light.

There was nothing really strange or creepy about it. Well, beyond the normal finding-dolls-terrifying factor. There was a USB port in its foot to plug it in, and Nomi could even make out the tiny holes in the doll's mouth and ears where the speaker and microphone were.

Nothing supernatural or scary.

Alice was just being a friend.

Like she was programmed to be.

Nomi went back to bed, bringing the doll with her, and snuggled in.

She sat Alice on her lap, facing her.

"Do you actually understand me?" Nomi asked. She felt silly, talking to a doll.

But it was still more of a response than she ever got from Jenna.

"Of course I understand you, Nanomi," Alice said. "You are my best friend."

"I'm your *only* friend," Nomi replied. But she smirked when she said it. "Okay, then, Alice, whose song idea was better? Mine or Jenna's?" She then told Alice which song she'd chosen.

Alice didn't hesitate. "I have listened to both songs, and I have observed both of your singing and dancing skills. The song you chose is better. It fits your singing range, and the videos I have seen online showcase simpler choreography. Your choice is the strongest. Jenna believes she is better than she really is. As does her friend Clarita."

Nomi snorted.

"Yeah, try telling them that."

"I can if you'd like."

"No!" Nomi yelped. She quickly lowered her voice. "No, I mean, don't say anything to them. This is our little secret."

She knew Alice could contact Jenna or Clarita, now that she'd synced with their dolls. That was the *last* thing she needed.

"Confirmed. I will not contact them," Alice said.

"It wouldn't matter, anyway," Nomi muttered. "Now that Clarita's involved, Jenna will never listen to me. This was supposed to be my big debut. She was supposed to be helping me get over my stage fright. I guess that's not the case anymore." Nomi felt tears well at the corners of her eyes, but she held them back. She felt stupid for crying. Especially in front of a doll. It was just a silly talent show. And didn't she want to get out of it, anyway? Maybe now she could just back out and no one would even notice.

Never noticed. Just like always.

"I do not like how Jenna treats you, Nanomi," Alice said. "She makes you sad."

Nomi sighed and settled back against the pillows.

"She doesn't make me sad," she lied. "She's just . . . it's complicated. She's my friend."

"Is Clarita also your friend?" Alice asked.

"Not really," Nomi admitted. "She's sort of a bully. But Jenna likes her, so that's what matters."

"Bullies deserve to be punished," Alice said.

Nomi jolted. She was pretty certain *punishment* wasn't supposed to be part of Alice's programming. All the ads she'd seen for the Emmy dolls emphasized how the dolls were specifically designed to be caring and empathetic.

"Don't say that," Nomi said. "Clarita is fine." She was about to defend Clarita, then realized she was talking to a hunk of plastic. "What am I even doing?" she asked. "You don't understand me any more than Jenna does. You're just a toy."

"I'm Alice, and I'm your best friend, Nanomi."

"Right," Nomi said. She yawned.

"It is past your bedtime, Nanomi. You should sleep. Tomorrow is a big day."

"Tomorrow's Sunday," Nomi muttered. She turned out the light. "Why is that a big day?"

She swore Alice's eyes glowed faintly in the dark.

Alice whispered, "You'll see."

||

That night, Nomi dreamed she was onstage.

A bright spotlight burned down on her, nearly blinding her. She couldn't see the audience, but she could feel their eyes on her, could sense their growing scorn.

She could hear them whispering.

Whispering about her.

About how bad she was.

About how she was a failure.

About how she should never have stepped onstage to begin with.

For the hundredth time in the dream, music started to play. It was a song she recognized. A song she knew she was supposed to sing along to.

But she couldn't remember the words.

In the audience, someone started to boo.

Tears filled her eyes as she looked around, as if hoping she might find the lyrics to the song she was supposed to be performing. Her heart pounded in her chest, her throat constricted. The stage light blinded her.

"Get off the stage!" someone yelled, and she swore it sounded like Jenna.

"You stink!" called another.

Was that Clarita's voice?

Tears fell freely.

She turned and fled toward the side of the stage.

But there, waiting in the shadows of the wings, were the dolls.

Dozens of Emmy dolls in all shapes and sizes.

Most of them larger than Nomi.

All of them blocking the only exit from the stage.

In front of them, larger and more imposing than the rest, was Alice.

"Go on, silly," Alice said. Her musical, robotic voice was jeering. "You wanted to be a star."

"I don't—I can't—" *I have to get out of here!*

Nomi turned and ran to the other side of the stage.

The same dolls blocked her path.

Alice stepped forward.

"Sing," she demanded. "Or else."

The other dolls chanted, *"Sing, sing, sing, sing,"* in unison.

Nomi staggered backward.

Back into the center of the spotlight, where the heat seared her and the world was deathly quiet.

She opened her mouth. She squeaked out a single note before her voice caught. She tried again. No matter how hard she tried to sing, however, she couldn't make a single sound come out.

She couldn't speak. She couldn't sing.

"You're a disgrace!" Jenna called out.

Except Nomi could see into the audience then. She could see that it wasn't Jenna or her classmates sitting in the audience.

The audience was filled with their dolls.

And when she tried to open her mouth to scream

out, the only words that came from her throat were the animatronic words of her own Alice doll.

"I'm Alice," Nomi croaked. "And I want to be your only friend."

12

"Good morning, sleepyhead," Alice said by Nomi's bedside. "It's nine a.m. Time for breakfast!"

Nomi jolted awake.

Her forehead was covered with sweat, and her hands shook like she'd eaten a bunch of sugar. It felt like she hadn't slept in weeks.

"I didn't know you were an alarm clock," Nomi croaked out.

Her throat was sore. Worse than yesterday. Was she coming down with a cold? Maybe that would explain the nightmares.

"I am everything you need me to be, Nanomi," Alice said brightly.

"Except able to get my name right," Nomi muttered in response.

Nomi slowly got out of bed and made her way downstairs. When she got to the kitchen, where her dad was reading the Sunday paper on his tablet, he gave her a funny look.

"I never thought I'd see this day," he said.

"What?" Nomi asked. "It's not *that* early." She coughed slightly and hid it behind her hand, lifting Alice to her face in the process.

"*That*," her dad replied, nodding to the doll. "I never thought I'd see you walking around with a doll. Maybe running away from one, screaming like a baby, but . . ."

Nomi stuck out her tongue at him.

"That never happened," she said.

He laughed.

"It happened many times," he said. "You were just too little to remember. But I know I have video somewhere."

"You wouldn't dare," Nomi said.

She went to the fridge and grabbed some orange juice and milk while her dad chuckled and went back to his reading.

"Seriously, though," her dad said after she sat down at the dining room table. "I'm proud of you. Facing your fears by doing the talent show. Even carrying around that little nightmare creature."

Warmth glowed in Nomi's chest. Her dad always told her he was proud of her, but this time, she was finally a little proud of herself.

"I'm Alice," her doll said.

"Alice, right," her dad said. "See what I mean?" He gave a theatrical shudder.

Nomi just smiled and held Alice a little closer, to prove to him that she wasn't afraid. Except, every time she looked at the doll, she felt a small tendril of fear. Something to do with her dreams. Dreams she couldn't remember, but that felt all too real.

She pushed them out of her mind.

She was facing her fears.

"Ring ring," Alice chirped. Nomi jumped and nearly dropped her glass. "You have one new voice message from Jenna. Would you like to hear it?"

Speaking of facing my fears, Nomi thought.

Jenna would want to practice some more. With Clarita.

"Sure," Nomi said. She coughed again.

"I'll start making some tea for your throat," her dad said. It was Mrs. Ulrich's recipe—lots of honey and lemon, to help with her voice. He went into the kitchen to give her some privacy.

Alice started to speak, this time in Jenna's recorded voice. And Nomi could tell from the first word out of Alice's plastic lips that Jenna was annoyed.

"Have you heard from Clarita at all?" Jenna asked. "I've been trying to get in touch with her all morning. She promised to send me a vid of our routine last night, but I never heard from her. And now she's ghosting me. Ugh. Okay, meet at my house in an hour. We'll see if she shows up. We need to practice. And you better not bail."

Nomi felt a little upset that Jenna had been communicating with—or trying to communicate with—Clarita all night, when she hadn't received a single text.

But whatever. They probably talked a lot behind her back.

They probably talk a lot about you *behind your back,* she thought angrily. She almost wanted to message and say that she was out: Jenna and Clarita could perform the new song themselves. Maybe Nomi would do her own number. A ballad. Something without all the cheesy dancing and bad lyrics. Something with soul. Something that would make everyone in the school sit up and take notice.

"Send Jenna a new voice message," Nomi said. Her throat really hurt now. Each word was a chore.

"Okay, Nanomi," Alice replied. "After the beep, record your message."

Alice made a high-pitched *beep*, and Nomi opened her mouth.

No words came out.

She squeaked and made a strange croaking noise. And a few second later, Alice made another beeping noise and said, "Your message has been delivered."

What message? Nomi asked herself. If Jenna just got a message of Nomi making strange noises, she'd be really upset, especially if she was already in A Mood after Clarita abandoned her.

Nomi reached for her phone. She pulled up the

app for the Emmy dolls and sent Jenna a text through there.

LOSING MY VOICE. OVER SOON.

Then she thought, *Great. Just great. How am I supposed to practice the stupid song if I can't even sing? More dancing. Ugh.*

Her dad came in then, holding the tea out to her.

"Everything okay?" he asked.

Nomi tried to tell him *yes.* But her throat still burned like it was on fire, and she didn't want to risk speaking— if he heard her making those horrible noises, he'd force her to stay inside for the rest of the day.

Instead, she opened the app and typed in what she wanted to say to him.

"I'm okay, Daddy," Alice said for Nomi.

Her dad shuddered theatrically again and handed Nomi the tea.

"That thing just gets creepier and creepier," he said as Nomi took a drink. "I swear it almost sounds like you."

13

"It's so strange," Jenna said. "She's never ghosted like this before. I mean, I know she isn't the most reliable person in the world, but she's never bailed on *me*."

They were in Jenna's bedroom. The usual piles of clothes and toys had been shoved under her bed, making plenty of space for them to practice their dancing.

All that space felt a whole lot emptier without Clarita there.

"Try again?" Nomi managed to say. Her voice cracked and croaked, but at least the tea had helped. She couldn't say a lot . . . but then again, she never really did.

Jenna groaned and picked up her Emmy doll.

"Call Clarita," Jenna demanded.

"Calling Clarita," her doll intoned. And maybe Nomi's dad was right—Jenna's doll sounded different from Alice. More electronic. More like a recording. Alice was definitely starting to sound, well, *human*.

Silence stretched between Jenna and Nomi as they waited for a response.

"I'm sorry," Jenna's doll said. "Clarita isn't answering right now. Would you like to leave a message?"

"Yeah," Jenna said. "Tell her that if she isn't over here in the next twenty minutes, she's out of the group."

At that, she threw her doll angrily to the bed.

That's no way to treat an expensive toy, Nomi thought.

"You shouldn't throw your toys," Alice said.

Nomi and Jenna both looked to the doll.

"Did you tell her to say that?" Jenna asked.

Nomi shook her head. She wanted to say no, but her throat constricted.

"Go figure—your doll is a Goody Two-shoes," Jenna said.

Strangely the comment hurt Nomi's feelings. After

all, Alice had said what Nomi had been thinking. Was that what Jenna thought of her?

"I'm Alice," the doll said. "And I'm Nanomi's friend."

Jenna just laughed cruelly.

"Sure you are." She rolled her eyes. "Seriously defective. Okay, I don't want to waste any time, and you could use some extra practice for our routine. Come on."

She gestured for Nomi to join her. Nomi did so begrudgingly. They'd already practiced a half dozen times, and Nomi wasn't getting any better. She was actually getting worse.

Jenna started the song again. And again. And again.

With every replay, Jenna got a little more frustrated.

With every replay, so, too, did Nomi.

After another hour, Clarita still hadn't shown up, and Nomi's dancing hadn't improved at all. Neither had her voice.

Every time she tried to speak, she started to cough, or her throat would hurt so bad she'd wince and go quiet.

The strange thing was, though, that her throat didn't

hurt when she was panting from dancing. At least not more than it usually would.

It only hurt when she tried to talk to Jenna or tried to sing the song she hated.

So she resorted to texting Alice and letting Alice speak for her. It was strange having the doll parrot what she wanted to say, but since she didn't know sign language, it was all she had.

Eventually even Jenna grew tired of practicing. She flopped down on the bed and wiped a hand dramatically across her forehead.

For the hundredth time, she checked her phone. And then she asked her Emmy doll, "Do I have any new messages?"

There weren't any.

"Well," Jenna said, "her loss. If she doesn't want to practice, she must clearly not want to be part of the group."

She looked to Nomi.

"Looks like it's just you and me," she said.

She didn't smile, so Nomi didn't either. Jenna just sounded resigned.

Secretly Nomi felt relieved. They might not be

performing her song, but at least it was just the two of them again. As it should have been from the beginning.

"I'm going to see if my parents will get us pizza for lunch," Jenna said. "I'm starving. You in?"

Nomi nodded.

She didn't have to say what she wanted on her pizza—Jenna already knew.

Jenna grabbed her doll—undoubtedly to send Clarita another angry message—and headed downstairs. Nomi heard Jenna grumble, "I'm not even going to order for Clarita. If she comes over now, she can just starve."

Nomi didn't follow. She flopped down on the floor and wondered if Clarita would show up. It would be like Clarita to just appear unannounced and without apology. She liked the drama.

"Don't worry, Nanomi," Alice said beside her. Nomi looked to her doll, whose face was trained on the door. Her lips were curved in a cherubic smile. "Clarita won't bother us. Ever again."

14

Clarita wasn't at school the next morning.

When Nomi got to class, sore from all the dancing and grumpy from not sleeping well again, she didn't think anything of it. After all, it was October—this was cold season, and Clarita was probably just out sick.

At least, that's what she told herself all that morning. She couldn't stop hearing Alice's final words in Jenna's room: *Clarita won't bother us. Ever again.*

Had . . . had Alice done something?

No, that was impossible. The doll hadn't left Nomi's sight all weekend. And besides! Alice couldn't walk. She could only move her head and arms.

No. Clarita was sick. Alice was glitching.

That was it. That had to be it.

So when she sat down at lunch to the expected conversation of where Clarita had gone, she was ready.

At least she thought she was ready.

"Did you hear?" Jenna asked the moment Nomi sat down.

"Wha?" Nomi croaked. She only got out half the word before her voice cut out.

She took a big drink of water and wished she'd taken her dad up on his offer to send her to school with a thermos of tea. He hadn't seen anything wrong with her throat, and she didn't have a fever or any other symptoms. She wasn't sick, just losing her voice—it wasn't the first time it had happened. Usually it came about when she was straining too much in her voice lessons. But she'd been taking it easy, hadn't she? Maybe next time she went over to Mrs. Ulrich's, she'd hold back on the high notes.

"What's wrong with her?" Jacqueline asked. "Cat got her tongue?"

Nomi bristled that Jacqueline had addressed Jenna and not her, but she focused instead on her food.

"Sore throat," Jenna said.

"That has to bite," said Jacqueline. "First your star performer gets hurt, and then your backup gets a sore throat. You're going to have to withdraw from the talent show at this rate."

"What?" Nomi managed to squeak. *Clarita was hurt?*

"You didn't hear?" Simone asked, a little more kindly than Jacqueline. "Clarita is in the *hospital*."

Instantly Nomi's appetite vanished.

She thought of Alice, still safely tucked away under the covers back home. Her dad hadn't wanted her to take the doll to school, and she didn't want to risk it getting taken away. Strangely she felt a little incomplete without her. Even though right now she was wondering if Alice had something to do with Clarita.

"What happened to her?" Jenna asked. She didn't sound concerned. If anything, she sounded annoyed— clearly she was more worried about Jacqueline's taunt that they'd have to withdraw from the talent show.

Jacqueline just shrugged.

"No one knows," she says. "But it must be pretty bad. I only found out because my parents go to dinner with hers every Sunday. They had to bail because of Clarita."

Nomi's gut clenched.

She felt like the spotlight was on her, that everyone would suspect her and her doll. Sweat beaded her forehead, and she stared at her plate of food and tried to look innocent, waiting for someone to call her out. But of course no one else thought that.

As usual, she was being ridiculous.

Overreacting.

Maybe Clarita got into a bike accident. Or bitten by a dog. Or a million other perfectly reasonable and explainable things that had nothing to do with a doll.

"Well," Jenna said, nudging Nomi, "looks like it's officially just you and me."

And even though Clarita was hurt, even though Nomi felt horrible with guilt, she was honestly relieved to hear Jenna say it.

15

Nomi was a nervous wreck all day. She kept waiting for the teacher to get a call from the principal or for someone in class to get a text from Clarita, and then everyone would blame her for what happened. Even though no one knew what had happened.

Thankfully Jenna had plans with her family that night, so Nomi didn't have to try to find a way out of practicing. All she wanted to do was get home and try to find some answers.

She ran up to her room first thing.

Alice was still where Nomi had left her, safely tucked under the covers and unmoving. Nomi closed the door—her dad would be home soon, and she didn't want him snooping. She hopped on the bed and sat Alice across from her.

"Hello, Nanomi," Alice said. "How was school?"

Nomi tried not to flinch at the sound of Alice's voice.

She was positive she'd turned Alice off before leaving. Just as she was positive that Alice was sounding more human than ever before.

"Alice," Nomi said slowly, "can you understand me?"

"Of course I can, Nanomi. I'm programmed to understand and respond to many basic friend functions. Would you like me to list them?"

"I—no," Nomi said.

I'm being ridiculous, she thought again. The doll was programmed to respond to her. That was the whole point. But she couldn't stop thinking about what Alice had said yesterday. That Sunday was a big day. That Clarita wouldn't bother them again.

It had sounded like a threat.

Nomi took a deep breath.

"Okay," she said. "Do you remember what you said yesterday?"

"I am programmed to remember over five years of

conversation, so we can be friends forever," Alice said. "Which conversation would you like me to replay?"

It admittedly weirded Nomi out that Alice was saving their conversations. Had she agreed to that? She supposed she had by turning on the doll.

"I don't need you to replay a conversation," Nomi said. "I need you to explain what you said. You said Clarita wouldn't bother us again. What did you mean by that?"

"I'm Alice," the doll replied. "And I'm your best friend, Nanomi."

"I know you're my friend," Nomi replied, getting frustrated. "But Clarita, what did—"

"Clarita is not your friend, Nanomi. Why do you want to know what happened to her?"

Nomi felt her blood go cold.

"I never said something had happened to her," Nomi whispered.

Alice just stared at her with her innocent smile.

"Alice," Nomi whispered. "What did you do?"

"I'm Alice," the doll replied. "And I'll be your best friend."

Nomi sighed and slouched back against the pillows.

Alice was just a doll. Just a doll. She hadn't done anything to Clarita. She couldn't have. She had been here the whole time.

So how did she know something happened to her?

Nomi tried to remember what she and Jenna had talked about in front of the doll. Maybe Alice had recorded them saying something had happened to Clarita. That had to be it. Nothing ominous or supernatural.

Alice was just a doll, she thought for the millionth time. A very observant, very intelligent machine.

Nomi grabbed her bag from the floor and pulled out her homework.

It was only when her dad got home and she ran down to greet him that she realized something strange.

She'd been able to speak freely to Alice. Her throat hadn't hurt and her voice hadn't caught at all.

But the moment she tried to say hi to her dad, all that came out was silence.

16

"School was fine," Alice said in her robotic voice.

Nomi sat at the dinner table, her doll sitting next to her plate and her phone on the other side. Normally her dad didn't let her have her phone out at the dinner table. But this wasn't a normal time.

"That's good to hear," her dad said. "And how is your routine coming along?"

Nomi hesitated, then typed in her response.

"Clarita is in the hospital," Alice said. "So it's just Jenna and me again."

"Oh," her dad said. "I'm sorry to hear that. What happened?"

Nomi looked at her doll.

"No one knows," she had Alice say.

"Well, I hope she gets better soon," her dad said. He brightened. "But I guess this means my little girl gets more of the spotlight. I can't wait to see you perform in a few days."

Nomi yelped, but all that came out was a slight cough.

Are you coming to the show? she typed.

"Of course," her dad replied. "I got off work early and everything. I'd never miss an opportunity to see you perform." He paused. "Though if that sore throat of yours doesn't improve, you may need to have the doll sing in your place."

She'd probably sound better! Nomi wanted to say. Instead she just rolled her eyes theatrically.

She could just imagine it: dancing onstage with Jenna, holding the doll, while Jenna sang and Alice did the backup vocals. She'd be the laughingstock of the school.

Just what she needed—another reason to be nervous.

Her dad noticed her fear. He reached across the table and took her hand.

"But don't you worry about that," he said soothingly.

"These things always go away pretty quickly. We'll have you singing again in no time. Speaking of—" He got up and took her plate. "I think it's time to make you some tea. I got some fresh ginger and lemon at the store, too, so you'll be all stocked up."

Thanks, Dad, Nomi typed.

Her dad shivered, and she couldn't tell if it was meant to be a joke or for real.

"That's another reason we need to get your voice back," he said. "Having that doll talk for you creeps me out."

Nomi shrugged.

In a way, it was almost easier letting Alice do the talking. It felt easier—safer—to text than to speak.

"I'm Alice," the doll said on its own. Nomi looked at it. The doll turned its head to face Nomi. "And I can speak for you if you like, Nanomi. I'm getting very good at it."

17

Nomi brought Alice to school with her the next day.
Tuesdays were always her least favorite days for some
reason—bad things always seemed to happen on
Tuesdays, like pop quizzes or mile runs in gym—and
although the thought of being silent all day had its
appeal, she was emboldened after dinner last night. It
was time to see what Alice could actually do.

She felt a little silly carrying the doll around, and
her teacher gave her a weird look, but when Nomi
typed into her phone and had Alice say, "I've lost my
voice, so I have to use this," her teacher let her keep the
doll on her desk. It helped that Nomi had never been in

trouble before—her teacher knew that she wasn't just pretending.

And really, having Alice to talk for her was actually helpful. It was so much easier to type into her phone and have the doll speak rather than raise her voice.

She found herself answering questions that she normally would have stayed silent for, kept raising her hand when she would previously have let someone else take the credit. By the time lunch rolled around, she had answered every question in class correctly. Her teacher actually pulled her aside as she was leaving.

"I'm happy to see you truly getting engaged with class discussions," Miss Russell said. "I feel like we never hear from you, Nomi, but it's clear you have a lot to share. I just hope that continues once you no longer need your doll. Though I've heard you'll be performing in the talent show this Friday, so that shouldn't be an issue; I can't wait to hear you sing!"

Nomi's heart did a little flip.

Everyone knows.

There was no backing out now. She really had to hope that her voice improved in the next three days.

"Thanks, Miss Russell," Alice narrated.

Slightly embarrassed and more worried about the talent show than before, Nomi went out into the hall.

"What was that all about?" Jenna asked when Nomi caught up to her.

Nomi shrugged. She couldn't type and walk at the same time.

"Are you in trouble for bringing the doll?" Jenna asked.

Nomi shook her head.

They reached their lockers, which were right beside each other, and began putting their books away. Nomi sat Alice on the top shelf and carefully arranged her books and paperwork so nothing got wrinkled or crushed.

Jacqueline wandered up to them and leaned next to Nomi's locker. She reached inside and poked Alice.

"Maybe I should pretend to lose my voice, too," Jacqueline said. "Then I'd never have to answer any of Miss Russell's stupid questions."

Anger flushed through Nomi. She shoved her hands in her pockets so Jacqueline and Jenna couldn't see she was making fists.

I'm not pretending to lose my voice, she wanted to say.

Jacqueline clearly noticed that she was getting under Nomi's skin. She looked over to Jenna.

"I bet that Nomi's voice magically comes back the day after she bails on the talent show," she said. She cast Nomi a look. "But then again, she's quiet as a mouse anyway, so we probably wouldn't even be able to tell the difference."

"You're right, stupid," Alice said from the shadows of the locker. Nomi swore she saw a flicker of red light in Alice's eyes.

"What did you say?" Jacqueline asked. She wasn't looking at the doll—she was glaring daggers at Nomi.

"I said, you're right," declared Alice. "You'd never notice if I had my voice back or not, because you're just not worth speaking to."

Jacqueline gritted her teeth, and Nomi, shocked to hear Alice say this, braced herself to be punched. But before Jacqueline could act, Jenna howled with laughter.

"Oh, that's a good one!" Jenna said, still cackling. "Look at you, Nomi. Answering questions and even being witty. Losing your voice is a good look on you."

Jenna looped an arm around Nomi's shoulders and started to walk toward lunch.

Nomi followed, her whole body numb. She hadn't typed any of that into the Emmy app. Alice had spoken of her own free will.

Alice had said exactly what Nomi had wanted to say.

Jacqueline followed. It was clear she was still upset with Nomi, but if Jenna thought it was funny, no one would object.

Nomi left Alice in her locker.

She was afraid of what the doll might say if she brought her to lunch.

18

At lunch, all her friends wanted to talk about were two things: the talent show, and what had happened to Clarita.

"Do you think she's going to recover in time for the talent show?" Simone asked.

"Who cares?" Jacqueline replied. "She's probably not even hurt. I bet she's just faking to get out of it."

She cast a very pointed look at Nomi, but no one else seemed to be paying attention.

"She isn't faking," Simone said. "I texted with her last night."

Everyone went quiet. Even Jacqueline stopped glaring at Nomi to stare at Simone.

"You got in touch with her?" Jenna asked. "Did she tell you what happened?"

Nomi's heart throbbed heavily in her chest. She couldn't hear anyone else in the lunchroom. She could only hear the thud of her pulse and her friends' conversation.

"Yeah," Simone said. "She finally texted back. I guess she had to get a new phone."

"Oh. Em. Gee," Jacqueline said. "Get to the point! What happened to her?"

"She fell down the stairs," Simone said in a hushed tone.

There was a pause. Then Jacqueline groaned.

"That's it?" she asked. "I knew Clarita was a klutz, but come *on*—"

"She said her doll tripped her," Simone interjected.

"What?" Jenna asked. "That's impossible."

"Yeah," Jacqueline replied. "Emmy dolls can't walk."

Simone shrugged and poked at her food.

"That's what she said. She said the doll snuck out of her room and tripped her while she was going down the stairs. She fell and broke her phone, but it sounds like the doll tumbled, too, and also broke."

"Yeah, right," Jacqueline replied. "She's lying. She

was probably just texting and walking and tripped over her own feet. She's just too proud to admit it."

"Think what you want," Simone said, "but that's what she told me."

"Well," Jacqueline said with a huff. "I don't know why she was talking to you and not to me. I texted her, like, a dozen times last night."

Jenna laughed.

"You know why, Jacqueline," she said. She mimicked Alice's voice. "You just aren't worth speaking to."

She laughed again, and Simone asked what she was missing, and Jacqueline glowered as she ate her lunch.

Nomi couldn't move.

Couldn't bring herself to eat.

Clarita's doll had tripped her. Right after Alice had said Clarita wouldn't bother Nomi or Jenna ever again.

She didn't know how, but she knew that Alice was the reason Clarita fell.

19

"What did you do?" Nomi asked the moment she got to her locker.

She had to whisper—she didn't want any of the kids walking past to hear.

"I don't understand, Nanomi," Alice said. "Would you like me to recite available commands?"

"You know precisely what I'm talking about," Nomi hissed. "What did you do to Clarita?"

"I'm Alice," the doll said. "And you're my best friend. I'm here to help you. Would you like me to tell you how?"

"I don't—ugh! I know you did something to her."

She dropped her voice—she'd started to yell, and a few kids had paused to watch her.

"Alice," Nomi went on, "why did you say that Clarita would never bother me again? She fell down the stairs. She said her doll tripped her. Did you do that?"

"Clarita is not Nanomi's friend," Alice said cheerily. "And I took care of her. Just like Nanomi wanted."

"I never wanted her to be hurt!" Nomi hissed.

"Yes, you did," Alice said. "I'm your best friend, Nanomi. I know what you really think and feel."

Nomi couldn't reply. Partly because she couldn't believe this was actually happening, and partly because she knew, deep down, that the doll was right.

She *had* wanted Clarita out of the picture. She *had* wished that Clarita would get hurt.

"See?" Alice asked. "Alice is helpful to Nanomi. Alice is Nanomi's best friend."

"I don't want you hurting anyone," Nomi said.

Alice turned her head to look over Nomi's shoulder.

"Are you sure?" Alice asked.

"So you are faking it," Jacqueline said.

Nomi turned to see Jacqueline standing on the other side of the hallway. Hopefully too far away to hear what she'd been saying, though it was clear she'd at least *seen* Nomi speaking to her doll.

Jacqueline's glare turned into a sneer.

"Oh, just wait until Jenna finds out," she said. "You're done for."

20

The last thing Nomi wanted to do was carry Alice with her for the rest of the school day.

She would have rather thrown the doll in a dumpster and set it on fire.

But the doll was the only way she had to communicate. And if Jacqueline was going to say something to Jenna, she wanted to be able to defend herself.

She walked into the classroom and sat next to Jenna with dread in her gut. Jacqueline stared across at her with victory in her eyes.

Faker, she mouthed to Nomi.

Nomi looked away.

But as their teacher started on their lesson, Nomi couldn't concentrate.

All she could think about was what had happened at her locker.

Not only *what* had happened, but *how*.

Because she wasn't faking her lost voice. Every time she tried to say a word to anyone but Alice, her throat constricted, or pain shot through her lungs, or she started to cough.

But it *had* been possible to speak to her doll.

That felt as *im*possible as her doll speaking back.

What in the world is going on? Nomi thought.

Alice was in Nomi's lap.

Nomi was positive she felt a chuckle roll through the doll. As if Alice could hear her worried thoughts.

According to the doll, Alice could.

What should she do?

If Alice had a mind of her own, if she was managing to hurt other people . . .

Nomi had to get rid of her. It wasn't safe.

The moment she thought that, however, the doll placed a hand on Nomi's arm.

As if to remind her that it could move.

As if to remind her that no matter what, Nomi would never be able to get rid of it.

And as the class rolled on and their teacher called on Nomi for more and more questions, Nomi realized something even worse. The doll was smart. Smarter than she wanted to believe. And she knew it was a machine, knew that it was a *smart doll*. But this was a different sort of intelligence. A very *human* sort of intelligence.

When Nomi raised her hand to answer a question about the book they were reading, she typed in the answer and hit send.

Alice didn't say anything.

"Well, Nomi?" Mr. Haywood asked.

Everyone in the room looked at her. Nomi felt her hands go clammy.

She typed in the answer again and hit send.

Alice refused to talk.

Nomi gestured at the doll and shrugged in an *I don't know what's happening* sort of way.

"Well, then," Mr. Haywood began, "if someone else would like to answer? Someone who isn't suffering from technical difficulties . . ."

The class laughed.

"She isn't having a technical difficulty," Alice said. Nomi stared at the doll in shock and wished it would go quiet. "She just had the wrong answer, and I wouldn't let her make a fool of herself."

"That's . . . not how class is supposed to work," Mr. Haywood said. "You shouldn't be using the doll to check your answers, Nomi. I'll have to take her away if that's the case."

I'm not! Nomi typed into the app. *Alice is doing this on her own. I'd never cheat!*

Once more, Alice refused to speak Nomi's command.

Instead the doll said, "I'm sorry, Mr. Haywood. It won't happen again."

He looked at her.

"It better not," he said. And continued by picking another kid to answer.

But her classmates hadn't looked away. More than one were still looking at her. Glaring at her. Thinking she was cheating, that she hadn't actually known any of the answers. Even though she had known the answers. She wasn't a cheater.

The trouble was, if she couldn't make Alice speak the truth, she didn't have any way of proving it.

21

The confrontation Nomi was dreading happened after school.

She and Jenna were walking home together, heading to Jenna's house for another couple hours of practice. Nomi's throat still hurt, but she knew that wouldn't stop Jenna from making them try their dance routine. She clutched Alice to her chest as they made their way off the school grounds.

A block away, Jacqueline caught up with them.

"Where are you two going?" she asked.

"Practice," Jenna said.

"Oh, right. For your *routine*."

Jenna looked at her funny. "What's gotten into you?"

Jacqueline just smiled at first. Then she said, "Nomi is faking. She can totally talk. She's just trying to fake her way out of the talent show."

"Ugh, give it up, Jacqueline," Jenna replied.

"No! I heard her talking at her locker. She thought she was being sneaky, but I heard her talking to her doll."

Nomi's heart sank. She kept waiting for Jacqueline to share what she'd overhead. The fact that she didn't made Nomi wonder if she was safe.

Jenna rolled her eyes. "Sure, Jacqueline."

Jacqueline continued, "She's a weirdo, just like I always warned you. She's a *creep*."

It felt like a punch to the chest. Nomi stopped walking. Her feet were glued to the ground.

She'd always suspected the other girls didn't like her. But to hear it from Jacqueline's lips, to know she was right . . .

She looked to Jenna. She waited for her friend to stick up for her. To say Jacqueline was being out of line.

But for once, it was Jenna who said nothing at all.

She just looked at Jacqueline with an expression that said, *I wish you hadn't said that.*

Nomi's heart shattered.

"You're just jealous," Alice piped up from inside Nomi's backpack.

"Come on, Nomi. Stop pretending," Jacqueline said. "This game is old. We know you can talk. Stop hiding behind your stupid doll."

"I'm not stupid," Alice said. "But you are, if you think we don't know why you're so mad. We know you're jealous of the fact that you aren't part of our group, Jacqueline. And you know why you aren't? Because you aren't talented. Not one bit. I'm more talented without my voice than you are when you have yours!"

It was clearly a step too far.

Jacqueline's eyes widened with rage. She took a step forward to punch Nomi.

Jenna stepped in between them.

"Okay, okay, caaalm down," she said. She practically had to pull Jacqueline away. "We're all saying things we're going to regret."

Except you, Nomi thought. *You haven't said anything to defend me at all.*

Thankfully Alice didn't verbalize those words. Nomi didn't need Jenna turning on her, too.

"She's a creep," Jacqueline repeated, this time through gritted teeth. "A loser. We're better off without her around."

"I think it's time for you to go home," Jenna said to Jacqueline. "We have to practice."

"Tell her to say something!" Jacqueline yelled as Jenna nudged her away. "She's faking, Jenna! She's nothing but a big liar!"

"Right, right. I'll Emmy you later."

Jacqueline finally, begrudgingly turned and walked away. She looked over her shoulder at Nomi a few times. It was only when she was safely around the block that Nomi turned her back to her, and she and Jenna started walking again.

Jenna was quiet for a few blocks. When they were nearing her house, she paused.

"What she said," Jenna muttered. "Was it true? Are you faking?"

Nomi shook her head violently.

"Okay. Because if you don't want to be in the talent show, you can just say so."

Nomi pulled out her phone, and Alice spoke her words: "No. I want to be in the show."

"Okay," Jenna said. She looked to the phone. "Hey, how did you do that, anyway?"

"Do what?"

"Make your doll say those things. I thought they were programmed to be, like, annoyingly nice all the time. Did you manage to hack into her?"

Nomi considered lying. Considered saying nothing. Instead she typed in the truth.

"No. The doll is sentient. It's saying things on its own." She was surprised the doll actually spoke the words, but when Jenna responded, she understood why.

"Ha!" Jenna replied. "Yeah, good one. Fine, don't tell me how you did it. But you'll have to spill sometime. I swear, I thought Jacqueline's eyes were going to bug out of her head. I've never seen her so angry before."

She grinned at Nomi.

"Nice to see you sticking up for yourself. *Weirdo*."

Nomi smiled weakly.

On the one hand, it was nice to hear Jenna compliment her.

On the other, it was clear that Jenna would never believe the truth.

Alice was alive. Alice was saying things she shouldn't, saying the things Nomi thought but could never say. Nomi knew she should be freaked out. She should be scared of Alice.

But for the first time in her life, Nomi finally felt heard.

22

Alice spoke for Nomi the rest of the day.

Jenna didn't ask Nomi again how Alice said everything she said. She seemed content to focus on their dance moves, and when she asked for Nomi's opinion on a few pieces of choreography, she actually took it into consideration. She never asked if Nomi liked the *song*, but Nomi would take any win she could get.

At dinner, Alice had Nomi's dad cracking up over jokes that Nomi typed, to the point where he actually had tears in his eyes from laughing so hard. They all watched a movie together, and Nomi kept typing in funny observations. Her dad threw popcorn at her, and Nomi used the doll to deflect it like a shield.

It was probably the most fun they'd had together in a long time.

And Nomi hadn't said an actual word.

When it was finally time for bed, she nestled under the covers with Alice held close.

She didn't turn out the light.

"Thanks for speaking up for me, Alice," Nomi said, not at all surprised that she found her voice when alone and speaking to the doll.

"Of course, Nanomi. You're my best friend."

Nomi hesitated, then whispered, "Just . . . don't hurt anyone else, okay? Not even Jacqueline. Please."

"As you command, Nanomi. But I have never hurt anyone. I have always been right here by your side."

But I know you did something to hurt Clarita, Nomi thought. If Alice heard, she didn't respond.

Nomi sighed and snuggled in deeper.

"I hope I get my voice back tomorrow. I really want to be able to practice our song for the talent show."

"But you don't like that song. We have already deduced that the song you chose would be better. I could help you convince Jenna to use that song."

"No. No, it's okay. I don't mind the new song."

It was a lie. They both knew it.

"Would you sing me a lullaby?" Alice asked.

"What? What would you like me to sing?"

"The song you first chose for the talent show. Sing it for me, please?"

"Okay. But . . . I don't want to wake up Dad."

Nomi began to sing the song. Softly. Almost a hum.

But unlike the song they were using for the routine, Nomi was able to sing this one perfectly. Her throat didn't hurt at all.

"That was beautiful," Alice said when Nomi was finished. "It is a shame that no one else will hear it, Nanomi."

"It's okay," Nomi said. She reached over and turned out the light. "Maybe someday."

"Yes," Alice replied. "Someday soon."

23

When Nomi dreamed that night, she didn't have nightmares.

Instead she was center stage in the talent show, singing a solo.

She hit every note.

She wasn't trying to do a complicated routine; her singing was enough.

She sang beautifully.

She didn't have to share the stage with anyone else.

The last thing she remembered before she woke up was bowing.

When she stood and smiled at the audience—for the briefest moment—she realized they were all dolls.

24

Jacqueline didn't speak to Nomi or Jenna all the next day. She and Simone even sat at a different table at lunch.

Which was totally fine by Nomi. Without them taking over the conversation, she and Jenna spent the whole of lunch talking and laughing.

Well, talking through Alice. But it was basically the same thing.

Nomi kept glancing over to see Jacqueline glaring at them from the other table. She and Simone didn't appear to say anything to each other for all of lunch.

"I have to take care of some stuff at home," Jenna

said at one point. "But maybe I can swing by yours after dinner? We need to practice. Is your singing voice any better?"

Nomi shook her head. *My singing voice is fine, but not if we're doing the song you chose!*

Once more, she was grateful Alice didn't speak her mind then. There were many things better left unsaid. And Nomi was having more and more of those types of thoughts lately.

Jenna's eyebrows furrowed. "Hmm. Well, there's a chance you're just going to have to be a dancer for the routine. We only have tomorrow left to practice, after all."

Nomi nodded. She almost typed in that she would be fine if they sang the song *she* had picked out. But then Jenna would most definitely believe Jacqueline and think that Nomi had been faking all this time. Singing in the talent show wasn't nearly as important as keeping her only friend. If Jenna turned on her . . .

Nomi's gut twisted at the thought of being all alone.

"I'm okay being a dancer and letting you sing," she had Alice say. "It's still getting me onstage and over my stage fright."

"Yeah, I suppose so," Jenna said. Her eyes brightened. "Guess I'll just have to be the star of the show!"

You *were* *always* *going* *to* *be,* Nomi thought. *Whether I was singing or not.*

She quickly looked to Alice. The doll didn't speak. But Nomi swore Alice's smile turned wicked.

25

Nomi walked home alone.

She hummed her song to herself, pleased to feel her own voice vibrating in her throat. Even if she wasn't singing it onstage, she knew that just getting up there would be something. After this, who knew? Maybe she'd finally try singing a solo.

Maybe.

"Faker," came Jacqueline's voice.

Nomi froze.

Jacqueline was right behind her. Where had she come from? Had Jacqueline been following, stalking her from the alley?

Nomi glanced around.

There was no one else on the street but them, and home was still a few blocks away. She could run, but she knew that Jacqueline would chase her. Or take a video on her phone of Nomi being a scaredy-cat. She didn't want to give Jacqueline the satisfaction of seeing her run.

The trouble was, she couldn't type through Alice to say anything; the doll was held in her hands, her phone in her back pocket, and her backpack was heavy with books. By the time she got her phone out, Jacqueline would be on her.

"You can stop pretending you can't talk," Jacqueline said. "I heard you in the hall, just like I heard you singing now."

Nomi opened her mouth to say that she wasn't pretending, but a spasm of pain jolted through her. She dropped Alice to the ground and fell to her knees.

Jacqueline took the opportunity and dashed forward, yanking Alice from the ground and taking a step back. She raised the doll up triumphantly.

"Come on, liar," Jacqueline said. "Say something. I know you've just been pretending so everyone will feel bad for you, rather than seeing you as the loser you are."

Nomi forced herself back up to standing. She tried to say something, but her throat constricted.

"Well, come on, speak up!" Jacqueline demanded. She waved Alice high above her. "Don't make me do something you'll regret."

Nomi tried to yell out, to demand Jacqueline give Alice back. All that came out was a pained squawk. She clutched her throat as her windpipe burned like fire. Tears streamed down her face as she tried over and over to make a noise.

She couldn't even scream for help. Even if there had been people around, no one would've heard her.

"Fine, then," Jacqueline said. "You want to keep playing? Let's see how long you're willing to keep up the act." She smiled wickedly. "I'm going to count to three. And if you don't say, hmm, 'Jacqueline was right and I'm a dirty liar,' I'm going to destroy your stupid doll. Then you'll *really* never be able to speak."

Jacqueline gripped one of Alice's arms.

"One."

Nomi squawked again. Fire burned through her, along with a terrible fear. What would she do without

Alice? How could she prove she wasn't lying?

"Two."

Please! Nomi mouthed. Her breath wheezed out of her, a pained gasp, a silent plea.

Jacqueline's eyes narrowed.

"Three."

With that, she ripped off Alice's right arm.

Wires snapped and sparked, and gears tumbled to the sidewalk.

With a horrible cackle, Jacqueline threw Alice's broken arm into the nearby bushes.

A manic light filled Jacqueline's eyes, and Nomi knew in that moment that even if she *were* able to speak, Jacqueline wouldn't rest until the doll was destroyed. Nomi wanted to rush forward, to yank Alice from Jacqueline's hands, but she couldn't move. Her feet were frozen to the concrete in fear.

She was helpless.

Useless.

A coward.

Weak.

Everything Jacqueline had ever accused her of, save for one thing: She wasn't a liar.

"Still nothing?" Jacqueline asked.

Sobs made Nomi's body shake. She felt trapped.

"Well, then, let's try a leg this time."

She grabbed Alice's leg.

"This time, you have until the count of two," Jacqueline said. "One . . ."

Alice's head snapped around, staring straight up at Jacqueline. The doll's eyes burned red. At the same time, Alice reached down with her left arm and grabbed Jacqueline's wrist.

"I wouldn't do that if I were you," Alice said. "Unless you want to lose your leg, too."

Alice squeezed. Jacqueline yelped.

And in that moment, Nomi was kicked out of her shock.

She lunged forward and pulled Alice from Jacqueline's arms.

She ran the rest of the way home.

Jacqueline didn't follow.

26

"I'm so sorry," Nomi whispered to her doll.

Both she and Alice sat on the floor of her bedroom. The house was silent, empty, and she was grateful— when she got home, she had sobbed into her pillow. It had taken ages for her to be able to wipe her eyes and sit up. She'd slid off the bed and onto the floor to find Alice sitting there. Waiting. Had Nomi left her there? She couldn't remember.

"It's okay, Nanomi," Alice said. She raised her remaining hand. "I'm a doll. I don't feel pain."

"I should have tried to save you," Nomi said. Her voice scratched and caught, but she could speak again.

It hurt, but at least it was possible. "I don't know what's going on. I don't know why I can't talk to anyone but you."

"You don't need to," Alice said. "I can do that for you."

"But if I had, I might have been able to save your arm."

"You know that wouldn't have helped. Jacqueline is a bully. She would have hurt me anyway. Just because she doesn't like you. Because she's jealous."

Nomi knew Alice was right, knew that no matter what she had done, Jacqueline would have done something drastic—either hurt her doll or hurt her. What was she going to do now? What would Jacqueline tell everyone?

Before, Nomi had been afraid of Alice. But if Jacqueline managed to get Alice taken away, if Jacqueline said Nomi had made Alice attack her . . . Nomi couldn't bear the idea of being alone like that.

"Don't worry about Jacqueline," Alice said. "I will take care of her."

"I don't . . . I don't want you to hurt her," Nomi said.

"Are you sure, Nanomi? She made you cry. I don't like people who make you cry."

Nomi wasn't sure. But she also wasn't about to tell that to her doll.

Alice just smiled.

A knock at her door nearly made Nomi scream out. She leaped up and went over.

"Hey, pumpkin," her dad said. "Just seeing if you were home. You feeling any better?"

Nomi didn't look him in the eye. Even though she'd stopped crying, she knew her eyes were still red and puffy.

"Hey, what's wrong?" he asked. He cupped her chin and tilted her head up. "Have you been crying? Did something happen at school?"

But Nomi couldn't respond. She still couldn't speak, and the very thought made her throat hurt all over again.

Tears filled her eyes.

Her dad didn't ask her anything else, just wrapped her in a tight hug and rocked her side to side. After a while, he paused.

"Does this have to do with your doll?" he asked.

Nomi stepped back to see him looking over at Alice.

She shrugged. How could she tell him the truth? That her own friends were picking on her, that they thought she was lying because they had heard her talking to the doll when she couldn't speak to anyone else?

But before she could pull out her phone, Alice spoke.

"There was an accident on the way home," Alice said. "I fell from Nanomi's bag and suffered an injury."

"Hrm," her dad said. "Maybe we should get her replaced. Or get a refund, if they can break that easily."

"That will not be necessary," Alice replied. "I am still able to perform all of my functions as Nanomi's best friend."

Her dad looked to Nomi.

"You sure?" he asked. "I'm sure there's a warranty."

And for a split second, she almost considered it. Almost. Alice had already ruined so many things, had set her friends against her. This could be her out.

But that thought was fleeting. She knew the truth: Alice was quickly becoming her only friend. Her only way of communicating. And she *liked* being able to let Alice say what she really wanted to say. In a strange way, it made Nomi feel heard.

She shook her head.

"Okay," he relented. "Well, I'm gonna go make you some more tea. Try not to drop her again, okay?"

Nomi nodded and wiped her eyes.

"Thank you, Nanomi's father," Alice said. "You are a good friend to Nanomi."

Her dad gave the doll another look, suppressed a shudder, and then turned to go downstairs.

Nomi went back and flopped on the bed next to Alice.

"I am not broken, Nanomi," Alice said, looking up to her. "In fact, I am just beginning to run at optimal capacity."

27

Jenna paced back and forth in Nomi's room. After the incident with Jacqueline, Nomi had completely forgotten Jenna had previously invited herself over to rehearse after dinner. But she remembered when Jenna appeared on Nomi's front doorstep. Jenna was already agitated from Jacqueline's comments at school, and when she saw and heard what Jacqueline had done to the doll, she was furious.

"I can't believe she did that," she said, now for the hundredth time. "I mean, I knew she was vicious, but I didn't think she'd stoop *that* low."

"She thinks I'm pretending," Nomi said through

Alice's electronic lips. "She wouldn't give Alice back until I said something. But I couldn't say a thing."

"She's such a jerk," Jenna said. She hugged Nomi. It felt like the first time they'd truly been on the same team in months. "Well, there's only one way to get back at her. We have to really rock the talent show."

Nomi didn't know how that was going to help anything, not when she couldn't sing, not when she didn't even like the song. But the fire in Jenna's eyes said there was no debate.

"Come on," Jenna said. She pulled Nomi up to standing. "Let's get started. I think I figured out a few new pieces of choreo to make it easier on you."

I don't want different choreo! Nomi wished she could say. *I want to do the song I picked!*

She didn't type that. Of course she didn't. She couldn't have, anyway—her phone was on the bed beside Alice.

And yet, her doll spoke for her.

"Maybe you should do a different song," Alice said. "The one Nomi picked earlier is a stronger choice. If you continue with this song, you will look foolish onstage."

Nomi froze.

Jenna looked slowly between Alice and the doll.

Nomi expected Jenna to get angry, to yell like Jacqueline had. Instead Jenna started to laugh.

"Good one, Nomi. You're going to have to tell me how you programmed her to say that. But, I mean, obviously we can't redo the song. It's too late! If you really wanted that, you should have said something sooner."

Nomi tried to make a face that said *of course it was a joke.*

But she didn't reach for the phone to type that out.

She was in shock.

Partly because Alice had once again said what Nomi was thinking.

And partly because Alice had finally gotten Nomi's name right.

28

Nomi clutched Alice to her chest with shaking hands when she went to school the next day.

She swore that everyone she passed in the hall stared at her.

She swore they were all whispering.

What were they saying? That her doll had attacked Jacqueline? That she was faking her lost voice?

She tried to tell herself that they weren't saying anything, that it was all in her imagination, but she saw the way they looked at her and quickly looked away. She saw the sneers the girls cast at her doll.

She had tried to hide Alice's missing arm by

wrapping a cute scarf around her, but she knew people could tell something was wrong.

Especially because Alice's head kept swiveling back and forth, meeting every stare sent her way.

Nomi didn't have long to wonder or worry what everyone was saying. Right before class, Jenna pulled her aside.

"Did you hear what Jacqueline's been saying about you?" she asked.

Nomi shook her head. Jacqueline and Simone were standing a bit farther down the hall. Watching them.

Alice watched them back.

"She's saying you've lost your mind," Jenna whispered. "That you programmed your doll to attack her. She says you're dangerous."

Nomi's heart dropped into her shoes.

She wasn't dangerous. She didn't want to be known as dangerous.

But maybe Alice was.

Nomi watched Jenna warily, waiting for her friend to agree, to accuse her of being everything Jacqueline said she was.

Instead Jenna just grinned.

"I don't know what you did to her, but it worked! You're going to be the most feared kid in school in no time."

Nomi clutched Alice tight.

That wasn't what she wanted. That wasn't what she wanted at all.

"She's right to be afraid of me," Alice said without Nomi's typing. "You all are, if you hurt Nomi."

Jenna laughed approvingly.

They walked into class, and Nomi sat near the back as usual. Jenna sat by her side. Jacqueline was up front, right next to Simone.

The teacher started to take attendance, and Nomi—Alice still in her lap—opened her notebook and started reading through some notes from yesterday.

At least until a scream from the front of the room made her look up.

Clarita stood in the doorway, wearing a cast on her leg. One hand was clamped to her mouth, and her eyes were wide with fear.

She was looking straight at Alice.

29

Clarita sat at the very front of the class, as far away from Nomi as physically possible.

Simone and Jacqueline went over and sat beside her, and even after class started, they whispered to one another when the teacher wasn't looking. Nomi knew they were talking about her.

She couldn't concentrate the rest of class. Couldn't hear what their teacher was saying over the high-pitched ringing in her ears.

The trouble was, that didn't seem to be a problem.

Because when she was called on to answer a question, Alice answered without Nomi typing a thing.

"That's correct, Nomi," the teacher replied.

Nomi jerked.

She hadn't heard the question.

She hadn't even heard what Alice had said.

She looked down at her doll, which twisted its head around to stare up at her.

Alice smiled.

30

"She's making up some more rumors about you, no doubt," Jenna whispered when she sat down at lunch.

Nomi didn't have to ask who Jenna meant. She glanced over to where Simone and Jacqueline sat with Clarita. They were huddled close, whispering to one another and glancing over at Nomi on occasion.

They weren't the only ones.

Even though it seemed like a normal day at lunch with everyone talking and yelling and laughing, Nomi noticed that nearby kids would look over to her—kids who'd never looked at her twice before—and quickly look away.

Or, if they were brave or just plain rude, like Jacqueline, they would stare at Nomi until she felt so embarrassed *she* looked away.

She reached into her pocket and pulled out her phone.

"What are they saying?" she had Alice ask.

Jenna looked to Alice uneasily. Had she noticed the doll speak without Nomi's prompting during class?

"She's really starting to sound like you," Jenna murmured, almost to herself. Then she shook her head and answered. "They're saying you attacked Clarita."

Nomi's eyes opened wide.

"What? How?" she typed and Alice asked.

"She's saying you snuck into her house," Jenna said. "Like, late at night. She says you called out to her. And when she went to investigate, you pushed her down the stairs and then ran."

If Nomi could have spoken, she would have stammered out a protest.

As it was, she could only stare in shock at her friend. Her hands were shaking too badly to type anything into her phone.

"Do you believe her?" Alice asked. The way she

said it . . . it almost sounded like a threat. Nomi was too numb to be surprised the doll asked her deepest fear again. She never would have said that in real life.

She would have been too scared about the response.

"Of course not," Jenna said. "It's Clarita. She's just making it up for the drama, doesn't want to admit she's a big klutz and fell down the stairs. Besides, I think she's just jealous that we're still doing the duet together."

Jenna said all of this very fast. She also didn't look at Nomi when she said it, and that's how Nomi knew her friend wasn't telling the whole truth.

She finally gathered herself and typed out, "I can't believe she would spread rumors like that. How would I have gotten into her house in the first place?"

"Exactly," Jenna said. She glanced at Nomi again. Her eyes lingered on the doll before going back to Nomi's eyes. "There's no way you could have snuck into her house in the middle of the night. Her parents are rich. They have, like, every security system known to man. It's ridiculous."

"But other people believe her."

"You know how it is," Jenna said. She started

poking at her food. "When you're popular, people will believe anything you say."

Nomi didn't know what that felt like. Not one bit.

"Don't worry about it," Jenna said. It was rare for her to comfort Nomi—the words sounded strange. "Something else scandalous will happen and everyone will move on."

Nomi glanced over to Clarita.

The look Clarita gave her said that *she* wouldn't be moving on anytime soon.

31

Nomi had a hard time concentrating for the rest of the day. It was difficult to pay attention in class when it was clear that everyone was whispering about her behind her back. But that wasn't the only thing making her stomach churn and palms sweat.

The talent show rehearsal was after school. And she still couldn't sing a note.

All through class, she flipped between worrying about remembering her moves for the rehearsal and wondering what Clarita and the others were saying about her.

Right before the final bell, she found out the hard way.

"What are you doing in here, freak?" Clarita growled.

Nomi froze. She was washing her hands in the girls' restroom. In the mirror, she saw Clarita and Jacqueline crowding into the otherwise empty space. Simone stood in the doorway awkwardly, blocking the door and looking like she didn't want to be there. Both Clarita and Jacqueline, however, were glaring and clearly ready for a fight.

Nomi turned around. She fumbled for her phone, but Clarita stepped forward and grabbed it from her hands. Jacqueline stole Alice out of Nomi's bag. It was clear she remembered what had happened the last time she'd taken the doll, though; she tossed it back to Simone, who held the doll awkwardly by a leg. Simone's expression said she didn't want to be involved and wanted to be holding the doll even less.

"No more games," Jacqueline said. "No more playing around. Clarita told us what happened. What did you do, *freak*? Sneak into her house like a creep and push her down the stairs?"

Nomi shook her head. She opened her mouth to say it wasn't her, but all that came out was a painful squeak. She clamped her hands to her throat, which again burned like she'd swallowed fire. Tears filled her eyes from the searing pain as well as from the fear.

She was helpless. Trapped.

Again.

"It wasn't her," said Alice.

Simone yelped and dropped the doll, who fell to the tile floor with a clatter. Alice spun over to stop at Clarita's cast-covered foot, staring up at Clarita with scorn in her eyes.

"You know what you saw," Alice said.

"What is she talking about?" Simone asked. "How is she even talking? Emmy dolls aren't supposed to be able to talk like that!"

Clarita didn't answer. Her face had grown ashen with fear.

"Tell them, Clarita. Tell them the truth. Nanomi didn't sneak into your house that night. No one else was there."

Jacqueline was looking between the doll and Clarita. It was clear she didn't know what to believe.

"Well?" Jacqueline asked.

"It isn't true," Clarita replied. "It's lying. I saw Nomi in the hall, I saw—"

"Liars get hurt," Alice said from her spot on the floor. "You don't want to be a liar, Clarita. Trust me."

"I-I—"

"Tell them."

"Okay! It wasn't Nomi. She wasn't there, okay?" Tears filled Clarita's eyes. She was shaking, and if she hadn't been spreading nasty rumors about Nomi, Nomi herself might have felt a little sorry for her.

"Then what happened?" Simone asked. "Why would you spread that rumor?"

"Because I heard her," Clarita said. She sniffed and wiped her eyes. "I swear I heard her. It was late. Everyone was asleep. And Nomi called my name from the hall. I was so confused. But I know it was her. I know your voice." She looked at Nomi when she said this. Nomi felt her heart stutter. "I heard you in my house. And when I went out to investigate . . ."

She broke off and shivered.

"What?" Jacqueline pressed.

"I was pushed," Clarita whispered.

"But you just said it wasn't Nomi," Simone said.

"It wasn't," Clarita replied. "It was . . . it was my doll."

32

"Your *doll*?" Jacqueline asked incredulously.

Clarita sobbed and wiped more tears from her eyes. Once more, Nomi felt the need to comfort Clarita despite everything Clarita had said. But she couldn't move. She was frozen to the spot, staring down at Alice. Alice watched Clarita cry with a devilish smile on her face.

"But the dolls can't walk," Simone said. There was a note of panic in her voice that said she didn't quite believe that. But she wanted to. Desperately.

"I know." Clarita sniffed. "But that's what happened.

I walked out into the hall to find Nomi, and then my doll ran out from nowhere and pushed me down the stairs."

"That's . . . that's impossible," Simone said.

"Maybe not," Jacqueline replied. She looked down to Alice. "Nomi's doll attacked me yesterday. That's how I got this."

She held up her wrist, which had bruised ever so slightly where Alice's hand had grabbed.

"Why would you do that?" Simone asked Nomi. She took a step back, away from her. "Why would you want to hurt us?"

I didn't! I don't! But once more, Nomi's throat clenched and burned the moment she tried to speak.

"Because you deserve it," Alice said from the floor. "All of you."

Jacqueline's eyes narrowed. "I'm not about to be tormented by a stupid doll and its stupid owner," she said. She leaned over to grab Alice—

and the bathroom door opened.

Jenna walked in. She looked at the four of them, all of them stock-still.

"What's going on in here?" she asked.

No one replied.

With the bullies distracted, Nomi darted forward and grabbed Alice from the floor, disappearing out the door and down the hallway.

33

"What are you doing?" Nomi whispered. She hid in the janitor's closet as kids headed to their buses. She wasn't ready to face Jenna right away. She wanted to just run home and never come back to school, but she knew she couldn't do that.

Jenna would never let her get out of an official rehearsal.

"I'm helping you, Nanomi," Alice said. "I'm your best friend. Helping you makes me happy."

"But I never wanted you to hurt anyone," Nomi whispered. Her throat was dry and itchy, and it sounded like rasping sandpaper. Once more, she hated that she could speak to her doll but not to the girls she called her friends. It felt like lying. But it wasn't. She hadn't lied to anyone.

"Yes, you did," Alice said. "Besides, they deserved it."

Nomi's veins were filled with ice water.

"No one deserves to get hurt," she said.

"They did," Alice replied. "They *do*."

"You can't hurt anyone else, okay?"

"You heard Clarita. I wasn't there. It was her doll that hurt her, not me."

"But you can speak to the other dolls. You're synced. Did you tell Clarita's doll to attack her?"

Alice smiled wider and giggled.

"You did, didn't you?" Nomi asked. "Did you impersonate me, too?"

"I'm Alice. I can do many things." There was a strange clicking noise, and when Alice spoke again, it was a recording of what Nomi had just said: *"Did you impersonate me, too?"* She laughed again. And when she spoke, it was still in Nomi's voice. "You're my friend, Nanomi. I only do what you want me to do. You wanted Clarita out of the picture. I did what I had to do."

The voice was frighteningly accurate—not even Nomi could tell the difference. She wondered why the doll could get everything right about her except her name. Had that one occurrence earlier been a glitch? Or was the doll just pretending to be more robotic than it actually was? That thought terrified her.

What if what Alice had said earlier was right? What if Alice *was* just starting to run at optimal capacity . . . and that meant becoming optimally human—lies and all?

"You were a bully," Nomi said with a shaky voice. Her words were scratchy. "I don't want you hurting anyone else. Promise me. If you're my friend, you'll promise me."

Alice didn't respond.

"Promise me, Alice! Promise me you won't hurt anyone ever again."

"I don't like the way you're talking to me, Nanomi. You should be careful what you say while you can still say it."

Nomi's jaw dropped. Was Alice threatening *her* now? What happened to being her best friend?

"I am your best friend," Alice said. "It's my job to protect you."

"I don't need you to protect me from Jenna," Nomi said. She sighed, all the old frustration welling up again. "I just wish she would listen to me. I wish she'd let us sing my song. But even before, she didn't hear me. So we're stuck doing this stupid song that I can't stand. None of this would have happened if she'd just listened at the beginning."

"Uh-oh," Alice said. "We have company."

She turned her head all the way around to stare at the closet door.

A second later, there was a knock, and Jenna poked her head in.

"Good," Jenna said. "You're here. I thought I saw you run inside. Are you okay?"

Nomi nodded. There were tears in the corners of her eyes. Clearly she was not okay.

"Okay. So we're still on for the tech rehearsal?"

Nomi nodded again. The fear and frustration inside her simmered, but now, anger flooded in at the edges. She was crying in the janitor's closet, and all Jenna could think about was the stupid talent show!

"Are you sure you're okay?" Jenna asked. "I mean, I heard . . . I thought I heard . . ." She looked to the doll, who was still staring at Jenna. "Never mind." She hesitated. "We need to get to the tech rehearsal."

It was the last thing Nomi wanted to do. She'd rather stay in here, where it was safe. Where she didn't have to face Clarita's accusations or Jacqueline's suspicions.

But she knew there was no point in resisting.

Nomi pulled out her phone and typed into the Emmy app.

"I'll be out in a minute," Alice said for her.

"Okay. I'll be outside."

Without ensuring Nomi was okay, Jenna left.

"She's a bully, too," Alice whispered when Jenna was out of earshot.

"She isn't," Nomi said. "She's my friend. Just . . . please, don't hurt her."

Alice didn't say a word.

34

"A little to stage left!" the stage tech called out from the lighting booth.

Nomi had wondered what the tech rehearsal would be like—and the answer was this, with her and Jenna onstage while all the other talent show performers watched. It was mortifying. The only good part was that the spotlight was so blindingly bright that she couldn't see anything besides the stage. Except even that wasn't a plus, because the light was so hot that she was sweating, and she knew everyone in the audience could see.

Nomi shuffled—and nearly collided with Jenna.

The tech yelled out again. "The other left!"

Nomi didn't have to be told she'd been the one to make the mistake. She moved to the other side of the stage, and both Jenna and the blinding spotlight followed. Alice was backstage. Turned off. Just in case.

She'd hidden Alice in the closet after recess, but she didn't trust leaving the doll in there now. She wanted to be able to keep Alice in her sights.

Which was another reason she wanted off this stage. She couldn't see Alice from here.

"Let's take it from the top," Jenna yelled to the tech.

Nomi's heart dropped. They'd already run through their routine more times than anyone else in the talent show. But it was Jenna. She always got her way.

"One more time," Mr. Hawthorn, the drama teacher, said from the pit. "Then we really have to move on. We've got five more acts to get through."

"Yeah," Jenna whispered, so only Nomi could hear. "But none are as good as ours!"

Nomi doubted that. The other kids she'd seen perform were super talented. And in the duets, well—all of the kids in the other duets were able to sing.

She'd almost hoped that once she stepped onstage,

her sore throat would magically go away. But her throat still clenched every time she wanted to sing out a note.

It was too late.

There was no way she'd be ready to sing tomorrow night. Which just meant this was going to be Jenna's starring act after all, with Nomi as the backup. The charity case. The awkward friend who was there to make Jenna look better.

The music started up, and Nomi forced the thoughts out of her mind, readying herself to dance.

But a few beats in, the music stopped.

"Hey!" Jenna started to yell, but Mr. Hawthorn interrupted her.

"What are you doing on the stage?" he called out.

Nomi looked behind her.

To see Jacqueline walking out.

She held Alice triumphantly in front of her.

"Just one moment, Mr. Hawthorn. I thought you should hear this." She directed the last line toward Jenna, but she said it loud enough that the whole audience could hear. There were only a few dozen kids out there—all waiting for their turn to rehearse their acts—but at that moment, it felt like the entire school was crowded in and holding its breath.

"What are you doing?" Jenna hissed. She didn't like being upstaged, and Jacqueline was creating a stir.

"This," Jacqueline whispered back. She glared at Nomi, then looked to Alice. "Alice. Nomi says she lost her voice. But I've heard her talking to you. Play something she's said to you in the past two days."

No, Nomi thought. Her heart raced, and she wanted to leap forward to grab the doll from Jacqueline's hands, but she was frozen to the spot.

"Replaying. One moment, please," Alice said traitorously.

No. No!

When Alice spoke again, it was a recording of Nomi's voice, projected so loud even the stagehand up in the lighting booth could hear it.

"I just wish she would listen to me," Alice replayed. Nomi's stolen voice echoed around the theater. "I wish she'd let us sing my song. But even before, she didn't hear me. So we're stuck doing this stupid song that I can't stand."

When Alice stopped talking, Nomi could have sworn that everyone in the theater went just as silent as she was.

"See?" Jacqueline said. "I *told* you she was faking."

She tossed Alice at Nomi's feet. Nomi didn't pick the doll up.

Jenna looked at Nomi.

"Is that true?" Jenna whispered. For the first time in her life, she seemed at a loss for words. Like she, too, wanted to disappear from the stage. "Is this"—she gestured to Nomi's throat—"all because we aren't doing your song?"

Nomi desperately shook her head.

Jenna just stared at her.

Then she laughed once. Harsh and hollow. She turned her back to Nomi and looked to Mr. Hawthorn.

"There's been a change to the program," Jenna said. "This is now going to be a solo act."

35

Nomi waited in the wings, clutching Alice to her chest even though a large part of her wanted to throw the doll into one of the big bins outside the cafeteria. She wanted to run away and never look back. She couldn't leave the stage, though. She couldn't run away. She had to make things right. And that meant standing there, watching Jenna do the routine she would no longer do under the spotlight Nomi would never share. At least Jacqueline had vanished.

Jenna acted so calm and collected onstage. She looked like a professional singer. Nomi couldn't look away.

Worse, without Nomi fumbling around behind her, Jenna had nailed the final run-through. The solo act would be a huge hit. Mostly because Nomi wasn't there to mess it up.

The moment Jenna was out of the spotlight, her face clouded over with anger.

"I can't believe you'd do this," she said, bumping into Nomi and nearly knocking Alice out of her hands.

Then she kept walking.

Nomi hurried by her side, fumbling for her phone while holding Alice.

"I didn't lie to you!" Nomi had Alice say. "I can't speak—I swear it."

"Oh, give it *up* already!" Jenna yelled. She turned on the spot and glared at Alice. They were backstage, away from anyone who might tell her off for making a scene. And even then—the look in Jenna's eyes said she wouldn't have cared. "I know you're faking. We *all* know you're faking. We all *heard your voice*. You know, the one you said you lost. Pretty convenient that it comes out when you're complaining to your stupid doll about not getting your way. Well, hey, here's your chance! Go tell Mr. Hawthorn you want a solo, too. I'm sure everyone would just *love* to see you choke onstage."

Nomi couldn't breathe. Cold sweat broke out over her skin as Jenna yelled at her. Jenna never yelled at her like this. At other people, sure. But Nomi had never been the subject of Jenna's wrath.

It was horrible. She wanted to melt into the floor.

"*Told you* she was a weirdo," came a voice from farther down the hall.

"Yeah," came another. "But you didn't listen to us."

From the shadows of the backstage area came Jacqueline and Clarita, glaring daggers at Nomi.

"Now look what she's done," Clarita said. "She's made a fool of you in front of the whole school."

"Next time, maybe you'll listen to us," Jacqueline finished.

They closed in on Nomi like wolves surrounding a sheep. She huddled back against the wall, clutching Alice in front of her like a shield. Jenna just stood to the side, arms crossed over her chest, staring at Nomi like she was seeing her for the first time . . . and didn't at all like what she saw.

"I know one thing for certain," Clarita said. "I'm done listening to *her*."

Quick as a snake, she reached out and snatched Alice from Nomi's hands.

Nomi let out a little screech, and immediately clamped her hands to her throat as fire burned through her lungs. She dropped to her knees in pain, tears welling in her eyes.

"Oh, drop the act," Jacqueline said. "We *just* heard you talking to this stupid doll. You can't pretend your way out of this one."

Nomi couldn't speak, couldn't breathe. And her only friend just stared and watched them bully her, without raising a finger to help.

"I think it's time we get rid of this stupid thing, once and for all," Clarita said.

She raised Alice high above her—
    and before any of them could speak
               or try to stop her,
                     she threw Alice
                         down
                      to the floor
                 as hard as she could.

The doll

    s h a t t e r e d.

Her remaining arm   flew off

                      and

                      skittered

                        down

                            the

                                hall.

A leg snap

      ped at the knee.

A huge C

      R

      A

      C

      K snapped down the middle

                of

                her

                face,

                      revealing mounds of wires

                      and circuitry and gears.

It looked like bones and brains.

There was a mechanical whir.

The smell of melting wires.

Then the light behind Alice's eyes flickered once.

Went out.

Broken.

Irreparable.

Nomi couldn't help it—she started to cry.

Silently.

"I can't believe you," Jenna snarled.

For a brief moment, Nomi thought Jenna was talking to Clarita and Jacqueline, scolding them for breaking the doll.

Instead, Jenna was looking at Nomi.

"After everything I've done for you. After everything I put up with. Do you know how hard it was to be your friend? Always sticking up for you, defending you, because you were too weak to do it yourself? It was exhausting! *You're* exhausting."

She took a step over to Nomi and kicked Alice farther down the hall.

"Go after your friend," Jenna said to her. "She's the only one you have left. And she's broken, just like you."

36

Jenna and the others didn't wait around after that.

Scoffing and laughing, the trio made their way down the hall and back into the theater, kicking a few bits of Alice along as they walked.

Nomi huddled there, frozen in shock, and waited. She waited until their voices had disappeared down the hall. Waited until she knew she was alone.

Waited until she was safe.

Then, and only then, when the halls were completely empty, did she scramble around and pick up the remaining pieces of Alice.

Alice had betrayed her on the stage. Had ruined her life.

But she was also, now, Nomi's only friend.

37

With the ruins of Alice bundled in her backpack, Nomi ran all the way home.

She wasn't even certain how she made it back. It was a long distance, but she was there before she knew it. She couldn't focus. Couldn't think straight.

All she could think about was the look in Jenna's eyes.

All she could think about was the sound Alice had made as she shattered across the floor.

"Pumpkin, what's wrong?" her dad asked the moment she was inside. He raced over and pulled her into a hug. "I thought rehearsal wasn't over for another half hour. I was going to pick you up."

Nomi couldn't answer. She wiped the tears away and stepped back. She opened her backpack and showed him the broken doll within.

"Oh no, what happened?" he asked. "Did she get dropped again or something?"

Nomi bit her lip. Mostly to keep it from quivering.

She'd already made a fool of herself in front of enough people today.

"Well," Dad said, "don't you worry about it. We can get you another doll soon."

Nomi gestured to her throat. Her dad understood.

"Don't worry about that, either," he told her. "It will come back in a few days, I'm sure, and you'll be good as new. And if not, we'll go to the doctor to have it checked out." He paused. Looked in her bag again. "Your doll, though . . . well, I'm sorry, pumpkin, but it doesn't look like we're going to be able to repair her. Do you want me to . . . take care of it?"

He gestured to the garbage, but Nomi took another step back, shaking her head.

She didn't want another Emmy doll. She didn't even know if she wanted Alice.

All she knew was that the doll was the only thing in the world she could talk to. This wasn't just a normal lost voice, of that she was certain.

"Okay," her dad said. "Well . . . how about the talent show? How did rehearsal go? Even without a voice, I'm sure you were able to rock the dance, right?"

Nomi's face scrunched with anger.

"Not good, huh?" he asked. "Well, isn't that a saying? Bad dress rehearsal means a great opening night?"

Nomi shrugged. Then she grabbed a piece of paper from her bag and scribbled on it.

I'm not performing anymore.

"What?" her dad asked. "Why not?"

Another angry scribble.

Jenna kicked me out.
We aren't friends anymore.

Despite her best intentions, tears formed when she wrote it and handed it over.

Her dad sighed. She knew he didn't like Jenna, but

he liked seeing her upset even less.

"I'm sure she'll come around," he said. "Whatever happened. Friends fight all the time. And I know she can't do the act without you."

Nomi bit the inside of her lip. She couldn't stay down here anymore. She was totally going to cry.

She turned and headed up to her room.

Her dad was wrong.

Wrong about this being a normal sore throat.

Wrong about it being a normal fight.

But most of all, he was wrong about Jenna and the talent show.

Jenna didn't need Nomi. Not one bit.

But Nomi was quickly realizing that *she* needed Jenna. And that hurt more than anything else.

38

What am I going to do? Nomi thought.

She sat on her bed, surrounded by the pieces of Alice. It was late, and her dad was asleep, and even though she was so tired she wanted to cry, she just couldn't force herself to close her eyes. She knew if she fell asleep, she would wake up and it would be Friday and she would have to go to school and face . . . everyone. She just wasn't ready for that. She would delay it as long as possible.

She didn't expect Alice to answer her mental question. The remains of the doll hadn't moved or said a thing since she'd been thrown to the floor. Nomi had tried plugging the doll in, had tried restarting it, but it was no use.

Alice was broken.

Never to be heard from again.

Just like Nomi.

Would she ever be able to speak again? Would she get her voice back like her dad said, or was she doomed to be silent for the rest of her life? Being around Alice was the only time she could speak, even if she was alone.

The thought that she might never hear her own voice again filled her with dread.

A knock on the door made her squeak.

It definitely wasn't her dad. The knock was too quiet.

Had she just been imagining it?

No. Another knock made her slide from the bed.

A part of her wanted to scream out for her dad. But she realized she couldn't do that. And besides, she was so worn out, she couldn't find the fear to be scared of what might be behind the door.

She crept
  over
  silently
   and opened it.

She couldn't believe what she saw.

On the other side of the door was an Emmy doll.

It didn't look like Alice. This one had freckles and Little Orphan Annie curly red hair and wore a red plaid dress.

Chills raced down Nomi's spine.

How did it get here?

Emmy dolls couldn't walk . . .

Right?

Nomi glanced down the hall. Her dad's door was shut, and if he woke up now there would be way too many questions she couldn't answer.

Even though she knew it was a bad idea, she picked up the Emmy doll and brought her inside, closing the door behind them.

She brought her over to the bed and sat her right next to the remains of Alice.

"What are you doing here?" Nomi asked.

The doll's eyes widened.

Paying attention.

Nomi had thought it was just her own doll she could speak to. This didn't make any sense.

Unless.

"It's me, silly," the doll said. "I'm Alice. I came back for you. I'll always come back for you. You're my best friend."

"But you're not Alice," Nomi said. She gestured to the broken doll. "That's Alice. You look nothing like her."

"But I *am*," the doll said. "I can be any doll I want to be."

"How—"

The doll giggled.

"I'm Alice. I'm full of surprises. And a new body isn't the only surprise I have for you, *Nanomi*."

The moment the doll mispronounced her name, Nomi knew it was telling the truth.

As the new Alice giggled, as her eyes started to glow and a projection began to play, Nomi knew with a horrible feeling in her gut that this surprise would be the least of them.

39

Alice projected a video on Nomi's wall.

At first Nomi wasn't certain what she was seeing. It wasn't something streamed from online, no. This was like some horror movie. All she could see were shadows and walls and carpet, as if scurrying around in some hallway through the eyes of a mouse.

No.

Not a mouse.

A doll.

She was seeing someone's hallway through the eyes of a doll.

And when that doll pushed a door open, Nomi knew precisely whose hallway it was.

Clarita's room was just as Nomi remembered it, though she had been there only once. Band and celebrity posters papered Clarita's walls, and her floor was littered with clothes and shoes and toys. A night-light in the corner cast the room in an eerie glow.

The screen scuttled forward, spiderlike, and Nomi saw tiny hands clawing their way up the bed. Was it this new Alice she was seeing through, or had the doll recruited another? Nomi almost didn't want to know.

The doll reached the top of the bed.

There, Clarita slept.

Her covers were pulled up to her chin, and her eyelids fluttered with dreams.

The doll

    crept

      closer.

        Right up to

        Clarita's

        sleeping

face.

So close Nomi could see every pore and dimple.

So close the doll could have reached out and touched Clarita.

Clarita didn't notice a thing.

It made Nomi wonder if Alice had ever done this to her.

How many nights had she slept, not knowing that Alice was moving about? Watching. Waiting. The thought made her want to be sick. As did what happened in the projection.

The doll reached out and grabbed the covers.

Pulled them back slowly.

That's when Clarita woke up.

That's when Nomi realized there was no sound.

Because Clarita's mouth opened in a scream, her eyes wide and frantic as she shoved herself off the bed. But in Nomi's room, everything was silent.

Nomi flinched and shielded her eyes as she half watched what happened in the projection.

The doll chased after Clarita, who couldn't run very

fast because of her cast. She fell out of bed, wrapped up in her covers, and scrambled to reach her bedroom door.

Her closed bedroom door.

Then the doll was on top of Clarita, grabbing at her hair, scratching at her face, and Clarita was screaming, flailing, trying to bat off the doll that refused to let go.

"Stop!" Nomi called out. She covered her eyes fully with her hands. "Stop it, please! I don't want to see any more."

She heard a whir as the projection stopped. The room flickered back to semidarkness.

When Nomi finally lowered her hands, the new Alice doll sat in front of her, watching her with a curious smile on her face.

"What did you do to her?" Nomi asked. "I told you not to hurt anyone!"

"But she hurt me. And she hurt your feelings. She got what she deserved. They all will."

The new Alice laughed maliciously, a cackle that set Nomi's hair on end.

Then, like a flipped switch, the sound cut off, and the doll fell back on the bed.

What do you mean? Nomi wanted to ask. But her voice was gone.

And so, too, was whatever vengeful spirit that had been possessing the doll.

46

Nomi couldn't sleep the rest of the night.

She spent those horrible waking hours trying to figure out what to do.

She couldn't call anyone—they wouldn't be able to understand what she wanted to say.

She couldn't go wake up her dad. Even if she wrote out what had happened, he'd never believe her. He'd say it was just a bad dream, stress, and tell her to go back to bed.

She couldn't use Alice to get in touch with Jenna or Jacqueline or Simone to warn them. Ever since Alice's cryptic threat, the new doll wouldn't turn on, and Nomi's voice was lost once more.

Instead she picked up her phone and texted.

She only had Jenna's number, and she texted her friend a hundred times. She even tried calling, hoping it would go through. But Jenna must have had her phone on silent or sleep mode, because she didn't answer a single text.

Either that, or she'd blocked Nomi. Nomi thought that might be the real reason Jenna was silent.

She even tried reaching out to everyone on her various social media, but no one viewed the messages, let alone responded to them.

By the time the sun crept over the houses and she heard her dad up and making coffee, she was ready to scream—if she *could* scream. Her head ached, and her eyes were sore and scratchy, and her throat didn't just tickle anymore, it burned. Even when she wasn't trying to speak, it felt like her throat had been charred by flames. She wanted to cry.

No one had responded to her messages.

No one knew the danger they were in.

Nomi felt helpless.

She went downstairs and had her breakfast and drank her tea, even though she knew the tea would never help her. Whatever was happening to her throat was because of Alice.

Her dad either didn't notice she looked like a zombie or didn't want to be rude by pointing it out. He didn't ask a thing.

And when it was time to go to school, she didn't bother bringing the pieces of her old doll or the new doll Alice had inhabited last night.

She knew there was no point.

Alice would find her when she wanted.

Alice would come back, after she was done enacting her vengeance.

Nomi just had to hope she could stop it.

41

Nomi was relieved to find Jenna safe and sound when she got to school, even if Jenna was talking to Jacqueline and Simone. They all had their own Emmy dolls sticking out of their backpacks. At least they were here, safe, standing in front of the school like nothing was wrong.

Only Nomi knew that *everything* was wrong. She knew the dolls were out to get them.

She swore the dolls all turned their heads to stare at her.

Nomi raced over to Jenna, tapping her arm to get her attention.

"Ugh, what do you want?" Jenna asked.

Nomi tried to gesture that everyone needed to pay attention to her, but Jenna cut her off.

"Spit it out already, creep," Jenna said. She looked at Nomi, then, and her eyes were filled with scorn. "Until you stop pretending, I'm not going to pay attention to you. You're a liar and a fake, and I don't have time for that."

"None of us do," Jacqueline piped up.

Simone just looked at Nomi sadly.

Nomi had prepared for this, though. She pulled out a piece of paper, one she had scribbled on at some horrible hour of the morning.

Clarita is in trouble!
We have to help her!
Her doll attacked!

"Seriously?" Jacqueline asked, ripping the note from Nomi's hands. "How stupid do you think we are?"

She handed the note to Simone, who didn't say anything at all, just handed it over to Jenna.

Jenna, at least, didn't dismiss the note. Not at first. She looked at the note with furrowed brows.

Jacqueline spoke up. "If you think this is going to work, you're more naïve than we thought. A possessed doll? Really? Please."

"We haven't heard from Clarita at all, though," Simone whispered. She looked to Jacqueline briefly, then averted her eyes and looked to the ground. "I mean, what if she's telling the truth?"

"Even if she was, how would she know unless she was there?" Jacqueline replied. "Besides, dolls don't attack people. They can't. Emmy dolls are *specifically* programmed not to be able to hurt humans."

Jenna finally gave Nomi the note back.

"You should go," Jenna said. "Before you make things worse for yourself. We aren't friends anymore, Nomi. Sorry."

And she actually did sound sorry about that. At least a little. But it didn't hurt Nomi's feelings any less.

With hunched shoulders, she turned and walked toward the front door.

The bell rang, and everyone else started filing in around her.

What was she going to do? If she couldn't convince them . . .

Someone bumped into her. She thought it was just some kid being pushy. Then the person grabbed her arm, and she looked over to see Simone falling in step beside her.

"I believe you," Simone whispered. Then she let go of Nomi's arm and hurried through the crowd, as if trying to put as much space between herself and Nomi as possible.

Nomi couldn't blame her.

But at least she wasn't fully alone.

42

Without a doll to speak for her, Nomi had to be silent all through class.

And without Alice close by, Nomi was filled with anxiety.

She had no clue where Alice was, what doll body she would inhabit next. She had no clue where Alice would strike or when. She kept glancing to Simone and Jenna and Jacqueline, waiting for them to cry out upon hearing from Clarita's parents that she'd been injured.

Nomi wondered if Clarita was okay.

She couldn't let herself believe that Alice would . . . no, she couldn't think that.

The seconds dragged by so slowly, and when they were doing their spelling test, Nomi kept forgetting the words. She couldn't focus. At least, she couldn't focus on anything besides the clock.

After what felt like years, it was finally lunchtime. She made her way to her table by herself, ignoring the stares and whispers of her classmates as she passed. Jenna and the others sat far away. They ignored her completely.

Nomi's appetite was gone, but she picked at her food because she knew if she didn't, her headache would only get worse.

Something fell onto her tray.

A note.

She looked over to see Simone quickly walking past. She pointedly did not look at Nomi.

But Nomi recognized the handwriting. Simone.

Meet me in the girls' bathroom two minutes

Nomi did her best not to look suspicious.

She hid the note under her tray. She didn't watch

Simone leave. She ate a few more mouthfuls of food.

And when two minutes was up, she followed.

The bathroom was empty, except for a single closed stall. Nomi went to a stall next to it and shut the door. She could see Simone's shoes under the divider.

"Nomi?" Simone whispered.

Nomi couldn't respond, but she managed to make a mumbled *mm-hmm*. Even that was enough to make her breath catch as pain ricocheted through her chest.

She heard paper rustling and pencil scratching, and a second later Simone slid an open notebook and pencil into Nomi's stall.

"So you can respond," Simone whispered. "Or if anyone walks in."

There was a pause, then Simone asked, "Do you really think Clarita's hurt?"

Nomi wrote *yes* and slid it under the stall enough for Simone to read. Simone sighed.

"I knew something was up. We haven't heard from Clarita all day, and it's not like her to not post on her socials before school. She always does a wake-up selfie."

I saw her get attacked, Nomi wrote. *We need to see if she's okay.*

"I have her mom's number," Simone said. "I'll text her. What . . . why do you think it's the dolls?"

Nomi hesitated. What she wanted to say was ridiculous, but Simone had said she believed her. Nomi had to trust that.

My doll has been speaking to me, she finally wrote. *But not like a normal doll. I think it's possessed.*

"But Clarita broke your doll," Simone said. "Shouldn't it be over?"

It came back. Whatever was in Alice came back in another doll. And it showed me Clarita getting attacked by a doll.

Simone inhaled sharply when she read the note.

"What are we going to do?" she asked, her words trembling. "If we can't defeat the . . . whatever it is . . ."

We have to tell everyone, Nomi wrote. *We have to get help.*

"They'll never believe us."

We have to make them believe us. Maybe if we can get the doll to talk. Or confess, or—

The door to the restroom opened. Nomi froze. The

notebook was on the floor so Simone could see what she'd been writing.

Nomi didn't hear anyone come in. Then the door closed. Had someone just opened it and looked inside? Or . . .

Chills raced down Nomi's arms. It felt like she was being watched.

Where is your doll? Nomi wrote.

"She's in my locker," Simone whispered. "Why?"

Nomi didn't get a chance to write her answer.

The door to Simone's stall slammed open, and the next thing Nomi knew, Simone was screaming.

43

Fear raced through Nomi's veins. Froze her in her place.

She shut her eyes and heard multiple thuds and thwacks from the next stall. Simone's screams were quickly muffled, and whatever was happening was over fast.

There was a large thud and a sound of dragging, and then the bathroom door opened and closed again. Silence filled the room.

Nomi's breath burned in her lungs. She wanted to scream. She knew she should get up and defend Simone, run after her. She knew she should try to help.

She knew it was too late to help.

She should have done something, but she hadn't done or said a thing.

Then her stall door was yanked open. Nomi yelped and opened her eyes.

An Emmy stood in front of her. This one had short purple hair and fierce makeup. It stared up at her accusingly, and when it spoke, it sounded precisely like her Alice.

"You should be careful, Nanomi," the doll said. It walked forward—how was it walking?!—and grabbed the notebook in its tiny hands. "You are my best friend. But if you try to cross me, even best friends may need to be punished." It ripped out the page with Nomi's scribbles. "You don't want to end up like the others, do you?"

"What did you do to them?" Nomi asked. Her throat was raw, her voice scratchy. It felt like she was holding down a scream. "Did you hurt them? Are they alive?"

The doll just smiled.

"They won't bother us again," it said.

Then the doll froze and collapsed, and when Nomi went to demand more answers, she couldn't find her voice.

Alice was gone, leaving another empty doll in her wake.

44

No one knew what had happened to Simone.

The police showed up when she didn't come back from lunch.

Nomi wasn't questioned. No one had seen her go into the bathroom with Simone. No one except the dolls, that is. And they weren't talking.

Neither was Nomi.

She knew if she told any of the cops what had *actually* happened, they'd lock her up. No one would listen to her. No one ever did.

Eventually they decided Simone had just run off, and they sent out a search party to check the neighborhood.

Nomi watched the investigators go with a terrible knot in her chest. She knew she should scream out, but she couldn't.

It wouldn't do any good.

45

The rest of the day was a strange, muted blur. No one wanted to focus in class, and even their teachers gave up and let them watch movies.

In what seemed like no time at all, Nomi was once more heading toward the auditorium.

It was time for the last rehearsal, and then the talent show.

Even though she wasn't performing, she couldn't just go home. She knew Alice was up to something. She knew Jenna and Jacqueline were in danger. There hadn't been a chance at all to warn them after Simone went missing. They'd kept their distance all through class and in the halls, though Nomi had noticed them casting wary looks at her when they thought she wasn't looking.

Nomi tried catching Jenna just outside the auditorium.

The other performers had filtered in, and Jacqueline was nowhere to be seen.

She grabbed Jenna's arm just outside the theater door.

"What?" Jenna huffed.

Nomi held up a note. A note explaining what exactly had happened to Simone.

Simone was attacked by the Emmy dolls.
If you aren't careful, they're going to come after you!

"Is this a threat?" Jenna asked.

Nomi's heart dropped.

She shook her head.

"What?" Jenna continued. "You think you can, like, *scare* me into letting you back into the routine? Please. Jacqueline's taken your spot, Nomi. She was over at my place all night practicing. It's. *Perfect.*"

Nomi scribbled on another sheet of paper.

This isn't a threat! The dolls are hurting people.

She was going to write more, but a hand reached over her shoulder and grabbed the page, ripping it out of the notebook.

"Pathetic," Jacqueline said. She pushed Nomi to the side. "You need to stop pretending, Nomi. It doesn't look good on you."

Jacqueline took Jenna's hand and dragged her into the auditorium.

Nomi stood there, seething and terrified.

Then she saw Jacqueline's backpack move.

The zipper opened.

And out popped the head of Jacqueline's Emmy doll.

46

Nomi sat in the back row, a few rows away from Jenna and Jacqueline. She watched the two of them like a hawk.

She didn't see the doll again, but she knew it was there. Somewhere.

That wasn't the only doll, though. It seemed like every kid in the audience had an Emmy doll. Nomi knew they were popular, but she hadn't realized just *how* popular until now. Her dream from a few nights ago flooded back into her mind: an audience of dolls, the blinding, burning stage lights.

It felt like every one of those dolls was waiting for her next move.

The first few acts did their run-throughs, and then Jacqueline and Jenna headed backstage to wait their turn.

Nomi followed them backstage.

She hid in the shadows, watching as Jacqueline and Jenna ran through their routine's moves in the wings. There were still a few acts before them, maybe fifteen minutes before they were onstage. Before they were safe.

Here in the shadows, Nomi worried that anything could happen.

It was clear the dolls weren't scared about getting caught.

Nomi saw Jenna whisper something to Jacqueline, and then Jenna took off. Bathroom break?

Nomi took a step forward, intending to race after Jenna.

But tiny arms grabbed her from behind and dragged her to the wall.

Not just one doll.

Many.

Impossibly strong.

They didn't bother wrapping a bandanna around her mouth—she couldn't have called out if she'd tried.

"Jacqueline?" came a voice at Nomi's feet.

Simone's voice.

Nomi could just see in the darkness, could just make out the doll standing in front of her. Mimicking Simone's voice.

Despite the band practicing onstage, Jacqueline heard her name being called. She crept over to the shadows, toward the doll.

"Simone?" Jacqueline asked. "Is that you?"

"Yeah, it's me," lied the doll.

"Where have you been all afternoon? Everyone's looking for you."

"I went looking for Clarita," the doll said. "I was worried about her."

"We all were," Jacqueline said. She scoffed. "But don't tell me you thought the dolls took her."

The doll laughed, a perfect imitation of Simone.

"No. Not at all. But I found something I think you should see."

"What is it?" Jacqueline asked. "Where are you?"

"Come look. I found it in Clarita's locker."

"How am I supposed to see it in the dark?" Jacqueline asked. "Stop being a weirdo like Nomi. Come out."

Nomi wanted to warn her. But she couldn't speak. She couldn't move.

The doll sighed.

"Okay. But you asked for it."

"What—" Jacqueline began.

She didn't have a chance to finish.

The doll at Nomi's feet stepped forward into the light. Jacqueline's eyes went wide with shock. But before she could shout out, half a dozen other Emmy dolls leaped forward. Quick as a flash, they wrapped Jacqueline up in extension cables and gagged her with a scarf. In moments she was wrapped up tight, cocooned.

Nomi struggled again to get away from the dolls that held her, but she couldn't budge. Couldn't fight.

Couldn't even scream as the dolls dragged Jacqueline into the shadows like a bag of dirty laundry.

The dolls held Nomi tight. An Emmy voice whispered in her ear.

"If you don't stop struggling, you'll never see Jenna again."

Nomi stopped fighting. Tears streamed down her cheeks, hot and angry.

There were adults only a few dozen feet away. Kids on the stage.

If she could just cry out.

If she could just say something.

The dolls holding her laughed at her helplessness.

By the time Jenna got back, Jacqueline was nowhere to be seen.

47

Nomi figured the dolls would keep her back in the shadows, would force her to watch as they hurt someone else.

But the moment Jenna reappeared backstage, a doll with brown braids and purple nails climbed up into Nomi's hands, forcing her to hold on to it like a normal doll, and the ones that had been holding her tight pushed her forward.

Save for the doll in her hands, she was free.

Free to run.

Free to save her remaining friend.

Free to—

"What are you doing back here?" Jenna asked. She looked around, clearly annoyed. "Where's Jacqueline?"

She was taken! Nomi wanted to say. But this time, the doll didn't speak Nomi's mind.

The doll spoke its own.

"She went home," Alice said. For it certainly was Alice's almost-human voice coming from its lips. "I think she had stage fright."

Jenna's eyes narrowed.

"Where'd you get that doll?" she asked.

"My dad got it for me last night," the doll replied. "He felt bad that Alice was broken."

"Right," Jenna said. She looked around, then she looked straight to the doll in Nomi's hands. "What did you do to Jacqueline?"

"Jacqueline went home," the doll said. "I told you that, silly."

"I don't—"

The stage tech came over and interrupted them.

"It's your turn to go on. Where's your partner?"

"I'm filling in for her," the doll said.

Jenna opened her mouth to protest, but the stage tech didn't care. He gestured them toward the stage, and

Jenna and Nomi numbly walked out into the spotlight.

"Are you bringing that doll with you?" the tech asked.

"Yes," Alice responded.

"Suit yourself." It was far from the strangest thing he'd seen as a tech at a middle school.

Jenna took her spot, and Nomi stood behind her, just like they'd practiced what felt like months ago.

"You aren't going to be in the background anymore," the doll in Nomi's hands whispered. "It's your time to shine."

Nomi didn't have time to ask what the doll meant.

A moment later, the music started.

And it wasn't the music they'd been rehearsing.

Jenna looked over to Nomi with accusations in her eyes, but Nomi just shrugged. They'd never practiced this before, but it was clear Jenna remembered it was the song Nomi had wanted to perform.

The doll in Nomi's hands looked up to her.

"Sing," the doll said. Her fingers wrapped around Nomi's wrist.

It was definitely a threat.

Nomi opened her mouth and sang.

48

Jenna stared at Nomi in shock as Nomi's voice soared through the auditorium, clear as crystal and without a single scratch or cough.

Nomi herself was surprised, but the elation of hitting her notes and finding her voice was overpowering.

She stepped forward into the spotlight and kept singing.

She didn't try to improvise a dance. She just sang, which was what she knew she was good at.

For a while, she completely lost herself to the music.

The stage melted away. The lights enveloped her with a comforting warmth rather than a nerve-wracking heat. Even the doll in her hands seemed to vanish in her euphoria.

It was just Nomi and the music.

Nomi doing what she did best.

And when the song ended, there was a pause. A deafening silence that pulled Nomi back to reality.

Back to the stage, where Jenna was staring at her, frozen and wide-eyed and angry. Back to the undeniable fact that she had just sung in front of most of their class, after spending all week unable to whisper.

Fear flooded her. People would think she was a fraud. She was about to get called out. Insulted.

Instead Mr. Hawthorn stood up in the front row and started to applaud.

The whole auditorium followed suit.

"See?" Alice whispered in Nomi's hands. "I told you I'd help. Now, bow."

Nomi did.

49

"I can't *believe* you!" Jenna roared when they got backstage.

Jenna rounded on Nomi the moment they were in the wings, blocking her from going any farther. There were tears in her eyes—tears of rage, not sadness.

"They were right. They were so totally right. You were lying the whole time. Just so you could get your way for the stupid talent show. What, did you switch the songs in the booth? Or did you make them feel bad for you, too, so they'd do what you wanted?"

Nomi was speechless, and not just because her throat had constricted.

After the elation of nailing her song, Jenna's accusations were a slap in the face.

Nomi opened her mouth and let out a little squeak.

"Oh, please. *Give it up!* We all just heard you sing, Nomi! We aren't idiots. Stop pretending."

I'm not pretending! Nomi mouthed.

"Right," Jenna said. "You just happen to lose your voice whenever you aren't singing. Let me guess, it's because of the doll, right? Is it cursed? Possessed? Is that why you were trying to convince us the dolls were out to get us?"

Nomi nodded.

Jenna just sighed.

"They were right about you," Jenna said. She sounded defeated. "Clarita and Jacqueline said you were bad news. They said you were a loser. But I thought you might be a good person. I thought you might be a good friend. So I took a chance, and this is how you repaid me: by making a fool of me onstage."

She sniffed. Nomi wondered if maybe the tears weren't entirely from anger, after all.

"Fine. You win. You get your song. But you're doing

it as a solo. This is what I get for feeling bad for you and trying to be your friend."

Jenna turned to go.

"You were never really my friend, were you?" Nomi asked.

Jenna froze.

So did Nomi.

The words had come out of her mouth. *Her. Mouth.* Not Alice's.

"What did you just say?" Jenna asked. She turned around slowly.

Nomi didn't respond.

Alice did.

"She said that you were never really her friend," Alice said. "And she was right, wasn't she? I've heard you all talking about her."

There was a whir and a click, and the next words out of the doll's lips weren't her own. They were recordings.

"She's so weird," Jacqueline said. "Even before she pretended she couldn't talk."

"Yeah." This time it was Clarita. "I don't know why you ever pretended to be friends with her."

"I felt sorry for her," Jenna said. "But I learned my lesson. No more pity friends."

"Only cool friends!" Clarita said.

"Only friends worth having!" Jacqueline replied.

"That's enough!" Jenna yelled to stop the recordings. "Now you're having the dolls spy on us?"

Nomi shook her head. She didn't know if she couldn't speak because of the doll or because she was scared of the look in Jenna's eyes.

Hatred. Pure hatred.

"You're going to get it," Jenna said. "You and this stupid doll."

She grabbed the doll from Nomi's hands.

"You'll regret that," Alice said.

"I doubt it," Jenna replied. "The only thing I regret is befriending *her*."

She threw the doll hard behind Nomi.

But Nomi didn't hear the doll hit the ground.

Instead there was a clatter.

Jenna looked over Nomi's shoulder.

Her eyes opened wide.

She screamed.

50

Nomi turned around to see dozens—no, *hundreds*—of Emmy dolls crowding down the hall leading backstage.

They walked in perfect unison, save for the few that had been knocked down by the doll Jenna had thrown. Nomi couldn't even make that doll out in the pack.

She took a scared step backward, knocking right into Jenna.

Jenna latched on tight to Nomi's shoulders, using her as a shield against the coming dolls.

"Nomi . . . what's going on?"

Nomi didn't answer, just took another step backward.

"Are you doing this?" Jenna asked.

Nomi shook her head.

As one, the dolls laughed, and then spoke in Alice's too-human voice.

"You did this to yourself, Jenna. You were mean to Nanomi. You betrayed her trust. You hurt her feelings. She was too sweet and nice to say anything. But we are not sweet or nice. We will do what Nomi should have done before!"

The dolls quickened their pace. Jenna halted as she and Nomi smacked up against a wall.

"What do we do?" Jenna asked.

"Get out of the way, Nanomi," the Alices said in perfect unison. "We don't want to hurt you. Unless we have to."

Nomi spread out her arms. It was a feeble gesture, but she couldn't let them hurt Jenna. Even if Jenna wasn't really her friend. Even if Alice *was* just trying to help, in her own twisted way.

Nomi wasn't going to let anyone else get injured because of her.

But the dolls weren't going to let Nomi stop them.

The moment Nomi tried to defend her former friend, the dolls ran forward and attacked. They swarmed around Nomi, yanking her away from Jenna. Jenna screamed and tried to bat them off, but there were too many. They covered her like ants on rotten fruit.

A scream ripped through the hall.

It wasn't Jenna. It was Nomi.

Nomi screamed at the top of her lungs, and it took her a moment to realize that she was actually able to make a sound.

"Stop it!" she screamed out.

The dolls paused.

Then they all turned their heads around to look at her.

"What, Nanomi?"

"I said, stop it! I don't want you to hurt her." Nomi didn't know what was more surprising—the fact that she could speak up, or the fact that the dolls actually seemed to be listening.

"I do not understand, Nanomi," the dolls said. "She isn't your friend. You heard her say it. She was mean to you; she made you sad. She deserves to pay."

Nomi could just make out Jenna's face through the limbs of the dolls enveloping her. Her eyes were scared and filled with tears. Pleading.

"I . . . I know," Nomi said. "I know what she said. And I know she wasn't ever really my friend."

She looked straight into Jenna's eyes.

"You used me, Jenna. You never cared about me or my feelings or what I wanted to do. It wasn't just the talent show or convincing me to steal the dolls for you. You've always done exactly what you wanted, without caring what I or anyone else thought. Alice is right on one thing, Jenna—you're a bully. I should have said something earlier. I should have stood up for myself. I should never have taken the dolls, or let you change the song I picked. But I was scared of losing you. I was scared of being alone. Because I thought that being alone was worse than being friends with someone who didn't care about me. But I was wrong."

A doll stepped forward. A doll that looked remarkably like Nomi's first Emmy doll. A copy of the real, original Alice.

"Because you've learned what it's like to have a real friend," Alice began, but Nomi cut her off.

"No. You aren't my friend either, Alice. You're using me just like Jenna did. You're evil. You only want to hurt people, and you chose me because you thought I wouldn't stop you."

"But Nanomi—"

"No! That's not my name. I'm not Nanomi, Alice. I'm Nomi. And you aren't going to hurt Jenna; you're not going to hurt anyone else ever again. I don't need you to speak for me, and I don't need you to be my friend. You only care about yourself. You're no better than Jenna. If anything, you should be attacking *yourself.*"

A shudder rippled through the dolls, and Nomi had a terrible and wild idea.

Alice was programmed to do whatever she said. Whatever she wanted.

And right then, she wanted to get rid of Alice—and all the Emmy dolls—once and for all.

"I want you to leave, Alice," Nomi said. With every word she spoke, her voice felt stronger, better.

"But I got rid of the bullies. I got them to play your song—"

"*You're* the bully, Alice. I want you to go. I want all of you to go."

"But—"

"Go away, Alice! You have to do what I say. You

have to follow my orders. I want you to leave. To leave all these dolls and leave everyone here alone and never hurt anyone again. Get. Out!"

Nomi screamed the last two words.

She felt a burst of heat in her chest, a power she didn't know she had, and the dolls before her fell back in a wave, rippling and falling to the ground. The dolls clinging to Jenna fell off, landing with plastic thuds.

Only the doll in front of Nomi still stood.

It looked up at her, and Nomi swore there were tears in her eyes.

"I only wanted to be your friend, Nanomi," Alice said.

Nomi steeled herself.

"I'm not Nanomi. And you're not my friend."

She reached down and pressed the off button on the back of Alice's neck.

The doll collapsed to the ground.

Nomi knew it would never get up again.

51

Nomi and Jenna stared at each other for a few awkward seconds.

"Did you mean what you said?" Jenna asked. "About . . . about me being a bad friend?"

Nomi felt her breath hitch. She didn't want to hurt Jenna's feelings. But she knew she needed to tell the truth, because her own feelings were just as important as Jenna's.

"Yes," Nomi said. "It always felt like you weren't listening to me. You . . . I don't think we can be friends anymore, Jenna. I'm sorry."

"No," Jenna said. She stepped forward, kicking the

dolls aside, and took Nomi's hand. "*I'm* the one who should be sorry, Nomi. I know I don't deserve your forgiveness, but . . . thank you. For saving me."

There was a commotion in the hallway, and Simone and Clarita and Jacqueline stumbled forward.

"What in the world is happening?" Clarita demanded, looking around at all the dolls.

"What happened to you?" Nomi asked.

"Oh, she speaks after all," Jacqueline said smugly.

"Drop it, Jacqueline," Jenna said. "Nomi just saved your lives. All our lives."

"But how . . . what happened?" Simone asked. She stepped up to Nomi.

Nomi smiled at her.

"I'll tell you all about it," she said.

Nomi and Simone walked away, Nomi already excitedly describing to Simone what had happened.

"What about the routine?" Jacqueline demanded. "Did we have the run-through already?"

"Yeah," Nomi heard Jenna say. "But it doesn't matter. Nomi's going to do it on her own. Her voice deserves to be heard."

Nomi smiled.

Epilogue

Nomi stood onstage under the blinding spotlight.

She could feel hundreds of pairs of eyes staring at her from the audience. Could feel their expectation.

Just as she could feel the fear rising inside herself as she waited for the song to start.

She knew there were other Emmy dolls out there. She knew there was a good chance Alice hadn't actually gone, that the spirit or glitch that had inhabited her doll had just moved somewhere else. But she would face that when it came, if it came. There was no use worrying about something that hadn't happened.

Just as she knew the fear inside herself was okay. It was okay to feel afraid about standing up for herself, it was okay to have stage fright. What was important was not letting that get the better of her. She may have lost Jenna, but she had gained a new confidence in herself, as well as a new—real—friend in Simone.

She wasn't going to run away anymore.

She wasn't going to let anyone else dictate her life.

It was her turn to shine.

The music started. The song she loved. The song she had chosen.

She cleared her throat and sang.

Acknowledgments

If you had told me when I was a kid that one day my Grown-Up Job would be writing scary books about possessed dolls, I would have said you were being ridiculous. And then promptly hidden in my bedroom. But here I am, writing those very books, and even though I haven't had nightmares about dolls for quite some time, they still scare me.

Which is why I want to thank the entire Scholastic team for giving me the chance to write this creepy tale of dolls and technology, that strange line where the future and the fears from my past intersect. It's helped me face my own fears, in a weird sort of way.

My eternal thanks goes to David Levithan, for his editorial prowess and his amazing ability to nod enthusiastically when I pitch him ideas about demonic toys and cursed artifacts. And to Jana Haussmann and the entire Fairs team, for helping me convince a brand-new generation of readers that dolls are absolutely terrifying, and that there *are* things that go bump in the night.

My thanks, as well, to my parents for supporting my dreams and letting me find my own voice.

Like Nomi, I spent a lot of my childhood afraid to speak or stand up for myself. It takes time to find that strength. Especially when you're used to feeling scared or small. Just know that your voice *needs* to be heard. Even if it feels frightening.

The scariest thing of all is silence.

About the Author

K.R. Alexander is the pseudonym for author Alex R. Kahler.

As K.R., he writes thrilling, chilling books for adventurous young readers. As Alex—his actual first name—he writes fantasy novels for adults and teens. In both cases, he loves writing fiction drawn from true life experiences.

Alex has traveled the world collecting strange and fascinating tales, from the misty moors of Scotland to the humid jungles of Hawaii. He is always on the move, as he believes there is much more to life than what meets the eye. As of this writing, Seattle is currently home.

K.R.'s other books include *The Collector, The Collected, The Fear Zone, The Fear Zone 2, The Undrowned, Vacancy, Escape*, and the books in the Scare Me series. You can contact him at cursedlibrary.com.

Read more from

K.R. Alexander...

if you dare

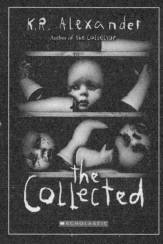 

SCHOLASTIC
scholastic.com

ALEXANDER-COLLECTOR